W9-CAO-740

The
Bell
Bandit

The Lemonade War Series: Books 1–3

The Lemonade War

The Lemonade Crime

The Bell Bandit

by
Jacqueline
Davies

Houghton Mifflin Books for Children
Houghton Mifflin Harcourt
Boston New York 2012

ACKNOWLEDGMENTS

Thanks go, as always, to the Gang of Four: Carol Peacock, Sarah Lamstein, Tracey Fern, and Mary Atkinson. A special thanks also to Kevin Sullivan of Paul Davis Restoration for providing information on home repair following a fire and to Lucia Gill Case for sharing the tradition of ringing a village bell on New Year's Eve. And thank you to Tracey Adams, the angel on my left shoulder, and Ann Rider, the angel on my right. To all the students in Ms. Amy Cicala's fourth grade class at Hillside Elementary, thank you for helping me with Evan's handwriting, especially Ryle Sammut, who wrote Evan's note for me.

www.hmhbooks.com. The text of this book is set in Guardi and Child's Play. The illustrations are pen and ink. Library of Congress Cataloging-in-Publication Data is on file.
ISBN: 978-0-547-56737-2 Manufactured in the United States DOC 10 9 8 7 6 5 4 3 2 1

4500349379

This one is for Ann Rider,
who always sees straight to the heart of
a book—and doesn't flinch.

Contents

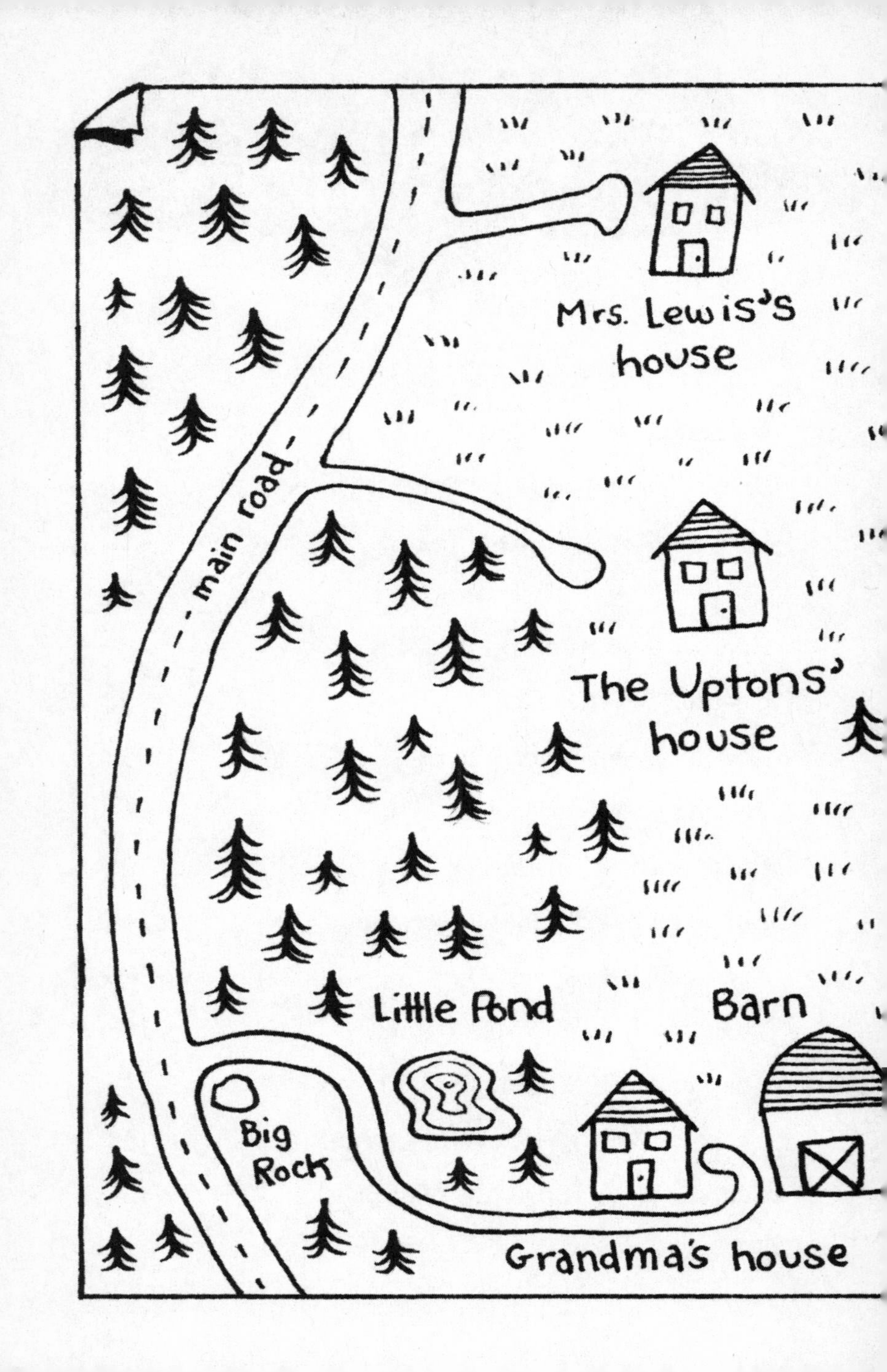
main road
Mrs. Lewis's house
The Uptons' house
Little Pond
Barn
Big Rock
Grandma's house

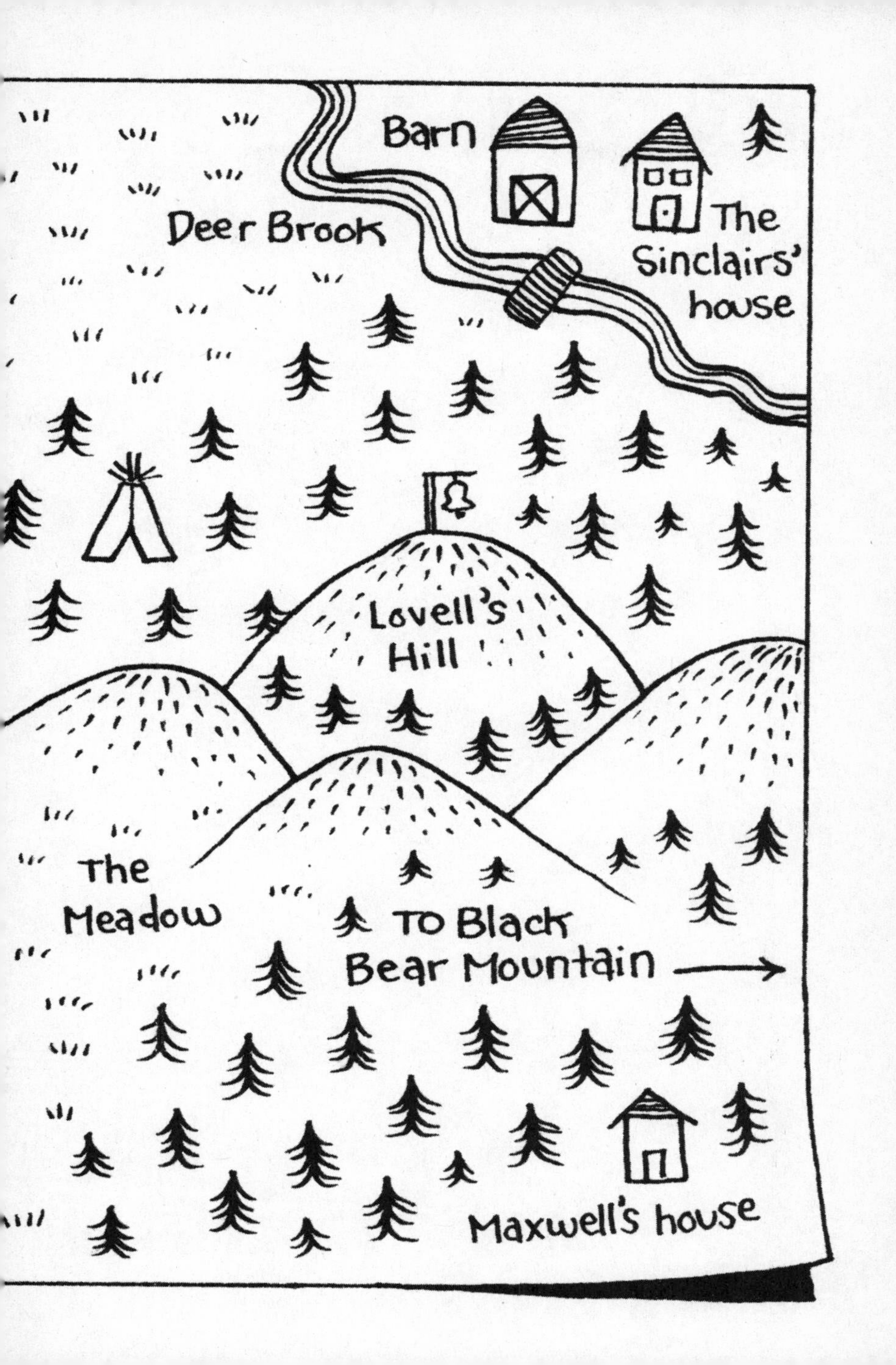
Barn
Deer Brook
The Sinclairs' house
Lovell's Hill
The Meadow
TO Black Bear Mountain
Maxwell's house

excerpt from

RING OUT, WILD BELLS
by Alfred, Lord Tennyson

Ring out, wild bells, to the wild sky,
The flying cloud, the frosty light:
The year is dying in the night;
Ring out, wild bells, and let him die.

Ring out the old, ring in the new,
Ring, happy bells, across the snow:
The year is going, let him go;
Ring out the false, ring in the true.

Chapter 1
Stuck in the Back

"How much longer?" Jessie asked from the back seat, tapping the window glass three times. Jessie always tapped the window three times when they passed under a bridge.

"Another hour," said Mrs. Treski. She glanced at the clock on the dashboard. "At least."

They had already been driving for three hours, climbing steadily higher and higher into the mountains, and Jessie could feel herself sinking into a sulk. Everything about this trip to Grandma's house was different.

First of all, Evan was sitting in the front seat.

Jessie could tell he was listening to his iPod. From behind, she could see his head bobbing slightly to the beat of the music as he stared out the window.

Evan had never been allowed to sit up front before. But this time when he'd asked—for the ten thousandth time—Mrs. Treski had given him a long, thoughtful look and said yes. He was ten and tall for his age, so Mrs. Treski said he was old enough to move up front.

Jessie was nine—and stuck in the back.

"Hey," Jessie said, trying to get Evan to turn around and notice her. But he didn't. He couldn't hear her. It was like he wasn't even in the car with her.

Jessie stared out the window at the farmland as it whizzed by them. Usually, she loved this drive. She loved to count things along the way—cows, hawks, Mini Coopers, out-of-state license plates. She kept tally marks in her notebook, and at the end of the trip, she would count them all up to see who had won. It was almost always the cows.

She also tracked their progress by looking for important landmarks along the way—like the pest control building that had a forty-foot fiberglass cockroach creeping over the roof, or the two-story carved wooden totem pole that was really a cell phone tower, or the billboard for a diner that had a big metal teapot with real steam coming out of it.

WHAT I SEE	LANDMARKS
cows ~~IIII~~ ~~IIII~~ III	☑ cockroach
hawks II	☑ totem pole
horses IIII	☑ teapot
sheep ~~IIII~~ II	☐ ladybug
goats I	
Mini Coopers ~~IIII~~ I	

License plates west of the Mississippi:

- Nebraska I
- Kansas I
- Idaho :)
- Missouri I

Evan used to be on the lookout for these landmarks, too, and it was a race to see who could spot each one first. But this year, he didn't seem to care. Even when the giant water storage tank painted like a ladybug came into view and Jessie pointed it out to him, he just shrugged, as if he couldn't be bothered. He was no fun, and suddenly the trip felt long.

They passed under another bridge, and Jessie tapped the window three times. "Why did Grandma set her house on fire?" she asked.

Mrs. Treski's eyes shifted from the road to the rearview mirror, locking on Jessie's reflection for a second before returning to the highway. "She didn't mean to. It was an accident."

"I know," said Jessie. "But why did it happen *this* time?"

Mrs. Treski tipped her head to one side. "Accidents happen. Sometimes there's no reason. She left something on the stove, and it caught on fire. It could happen to anyone."

But it hadn't happened to her grandmother before. Jessie thought about all the times Grandma had cooked noodles for her or made hot chocolate for her or heated up soup for her. Not once had she set the house on fire.

It was because of the fire that they were driving up to Grandma's two days *after* Christmas instead of the day *before,* the way they always did. And it was because of the fire that they weren't even sure if they would be staying at Grandma's for New Year's Eve the way they did every year. And that was the really big thing that was different this time.

For as long as Jessie could remember, New Year's Eve meant staying at Grandma's house and the long, slow climb to the top of Lovell's Hill, where the trees parted and the sky opened and there stood the old iron bell hanging on its heavy wooden crossbeam.

Just before midnight they would gather, walking through the snow-covered woods, coming from all sides of the hill—neighbors and friends, family and sometimes even strangers—to sing the old songs and talk about the year gone by.

And then, just before midnight, the youngest

one in the crowd and the oldest one, too, would step forward and both take hold of the rope that hung from the clapper of the dark and heavy bell, and at precisely the right moment, they would ring in the New Year, as loudly and joyously and for as long as they wanted.

Jessie remembered the year when *she* had been the youngest one on the hill, and what it felt like when Mrs. Lewis, who was eighty-four that year, had closed her soft, papery hand over hers. They had swung the rope back and forth, over and over, until the noise of the bell filled the snow-covered valley below and the echoes of each peal bounced off of Black Bear Mountain and came racing back to them, like an old faithful dog that always comes home.

But this year, everything was upside down. They might not even spend New Year's Eve at Grandma's house. It all depended, Mrs. Treski said. On what? Jessie wondered. She tapped her right knee twice. Not spend New Year's Eve at Grandma's? Who would ring the bell?

Jessie jiggled her legs up and down. Her left foot was feeling prickly because she'd had it tucked up under her for the last half-hour. "How much longer to the Crossroads Store?" she asked.

"Oh, Jessie . . ." said her mother, looking in the rearview mirror again. "Do you need to stop?"

"What do you mean?" asked Jessie. It wasn't a question of whether she *needed* to—although now that she thought of it, a trip to the bathroom sounded like a good idea. "We always stop at the Crossroads Store," she said, with a hint of a whine in her voice.

"It's just that I thought this time we could drive straight through," said Mrs. Treski. "We're making such good time, and you know how the weather is in the mountains. You never know what might blow in."

"Mo-o-om," said Jessie. Everything was messed up on this trip. "Evan, you want to stop at the Crossroads, don't you?"

Evan just kept looking out the window, nodding his head in time to the music on his iPod.

"Evan!" Jessie didn't mean to hit him quite so hard on the shoulder.

"Quit it!" he said, turning around to glare at her.

"I'm asking you a question!" she shouted. Evan took out one of the ear buds and let it dangle from his ear like a dead worm on a hook. "Do you want to stop at the Crossroads?" Jessie couldn't help thinking the question sounded dumb. Of course he would want to stop.

But Evan just shrugged and put the ear bud back in his ear. "I don't care."

Jessie threw herself against the seat and folded her arms over her chest.

"Relax, Jessie," said Mrs. Treski. "We'll stop. I could use a break to stretch my legs, anyway. But we can't stay too long. I don't want to get to Grandma's after dark."

* * *

The Crossroads Store was a ten-minute detour off the main highway. It was on the corner of two roads that were so dinky, Mrs. Treski called it the intersection of Nowhere and Oblivion. But the store itself was miraculous. It was a combination gas station, deli, bakery, gift shop, bookshop, hunting/fishing/clothing store, and post office. They sold kayaks, guns, taxidermied animals, hunting knives, Get Well cards, umbrellas, joke books, night crawlers, candy, and decorative wall calendars. Jessie could wander the store for hours, wishing she had the money to buy just about everything.

She had only five dollars in her pocket, though. That was all the money she'd allowed herself to bring on this trip. Back home in her lock box, she had almost thirty dollars. Most of that was from the money she'd made during the lemonade war, or at least what was left over after she made that $104 contribution to the Animal Rescue League. ("You don't have to give as much as I did," Megan had said, but Jessie had insisted. "I said I was going to, and I'm going to," she said, even though it almost killed her to give all that money away—and to animals!)

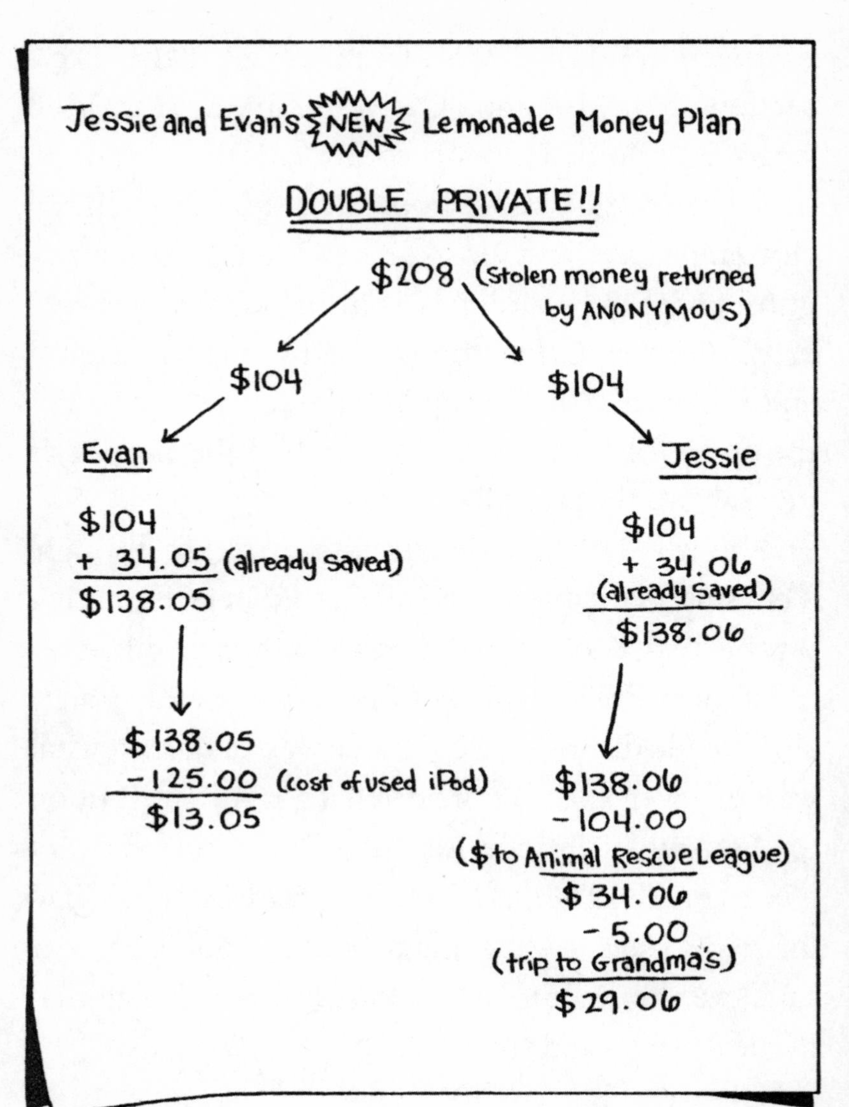
Jessie and Evan's NEW Lemonade Money Plan
DOUBLE PRIVATE!!
$208 (stolen money returned by ANONYMOUS)
$104
$104
Evan
Jessie
$104
+ 34.05 (already saved)
$138.05
$104
+ 34.06
(already saved)
$138.06
$138.05
-125.00 (cost of used iPod)
$13.05
$138.06
-104.00
($ to Animal Rescue League)
$34.06
-5.00
(trip to Grandma's)
$29.06

But no matter how enticing everything in the Crossroads Store looked to her (a squirrel nutcracker! fake mustaches!), Jessie wasn't about to spend thirty dollars. She liked to have money saved. Just in case.

After using the bathroom, she walked over to where Evan was standing, halfway between the deli and the bakery. He was looking at fancy gift bags of candy, all done up with curlicue ribbons.

"Look!" he said, holding up a bag. The label on the bag said "Moose Droppings." "Want some?" he asked, dangling the bag in front of her face.

"That is so gross!" Jessie said. But she loved it. The candy really did look exactly like moose droppings, only smaller. On closer inspection, she saw that it was actually chocolate-covered blueberries. "Are you going to get a bag? We could split one." But Evan had wandered off and wasn't listening to her anymore.

Jessie put the bag back on the shelf and walked over to the corner of the store devoted to jigsaw puzzles. There were a dozen puzzles to choose from, but Jessie's eyes went immediately to the one that was a picture of jellybeans. The brightly colored candies looked like rocks on a pebbly beach, and Jessie knew the puzzle would be hard to do. It had a thousand pieces!

"Jessie, are you ready?" asked her mother, shoving a few dollars back into her wallet after paying for the gas.

"Can we get this? Please?" asked Jessie, pulling the jellybean puzzle down from the shelf. "For Grandma?" Jessie and Grandma always worked on jigsaw puzzles when the family visited, and Jessie often brought a new puzzle for them to try. They had never done a thousand-piece puzzle, though.

Jessie's mom paused, the money still hanging out from her wallet. Jessie knew her mom had to be careful with money, and she tried hard not to ask for things she didn't need. "I have five dollars," said Jessie. "I could chip in."

Mrs. Treski took the puzzle and said, "It's a good idea, Jess. You and Grandma can work on it when she gets home from the hospital."

Jessie smiled, glad she could have the puzzle without spending her own money, and turned to the circular spinning postcard rack that was next to the jigsaw puzzles. There were eight columns of cards, and Jessie liked to make the rack squeak as she turned it slowly. She started at the top and began to work her way straight down one column, and then went back up to the top of the next column. She didn't want to miss a single card.

"Jess, can we go now?" asked her mother, looking through the various compartments of her wallet as if money would magically appear if she looked hard enough.

"No, I'm looking at the cards."

"You must own every card on that rack."

"Sometimes they have a new one," said Jessie.

"Five minutes, okay? Five minutes, I want to be pulling out of the parking lot." Mrs. Treski walked off to the checkout counter to pay for the puzzle.

Why was her mom so impatient? Usually she loved to stop at the Crossroads, but this time it was all about making good time and getting back on the road. Well, Jessie wasn't going to be rushed. She finished looking at the second column of postcards, and then started on the third.

"Ever been there?"

Jessie looked up. An old man with a stubbly beard was squinting through his glasses at a postcard that showed the Olympic Stadium in Lake Placid. Jessie noticed that the glasses sat crooked on his face. "The stadium where they had the Olympics? Ever been there?"

Jessie shook her head. "No."

The man tapped the card. "I was there in 1980 *and* 1932. Yes, I was. I saw Sonja Henie win the gold medal for figure skating. Do you believe that?" He nodded his head up and down as if he could make Jessie do the same.

Jessie looked closely at the man standing beside her. He started to scratch his face like he had a bad rash. "Were you in the Olympics?" she asked.

"No!" said the man. "But I had dreams." He was nodding his head more vigorously now—nodding and scratching—and his eyes were locked on the far end of the store.

"Hey, Jess, come on," said Evan, grabbing hold of one elbow and pulling her toward the door.

"I'm not done!" she said. But Evan didn't let go of her until they were outside. When Jessie looked back through the window, she saw that the man was still scratching his face and talking, even though no one was near.

"That guy was crazy," Evan said, matter-of-factly.

"How do you know?" asked Jessie, looking up at her big brother.

Evan shrugged and put his headphones back on. "You can just tell."

But Jessie couldn't tell. It hadn't occurred to her that there was anything wrong with the old man. Why did old people get like that? Did something break down inside their heads, the way a shoelace eventually snaps after being tied too many times? And how exactly did Evan know?

As soon as they got back on the highway, it started to snow. At first the flakes were large and wet, sticking for an instant to the windshield like giant white moths before dissolving into quarter-size drops of water. Then the snow became steadier and more fierce, and the ground on either side of the highway turned white and shapeless. It was dusk when they pulled up to the end of Grandma's long, winding driveway and got their first look at the house.

"Oh my," said Mrs. Treski, turning off the ignition and letting the car lights die.

Chapter 2

The Man of the Family

Normally, they would have walked into the house through the back door. But there was no back door. There was hardly even a back wall.

Evan couldn't believe it once they unlocked the front door and made their way through the dark into the kitchen. There was a hole in the back kitchen wall big enough to drive a car through. It looked like someone *had* driven a car straight through it, except that the edges of the hole were as black as coal and the smell of smoke was everywhere. Someone had taped heavy clear plastic to the wall, but one edge had come undone and was flapping in the wind.

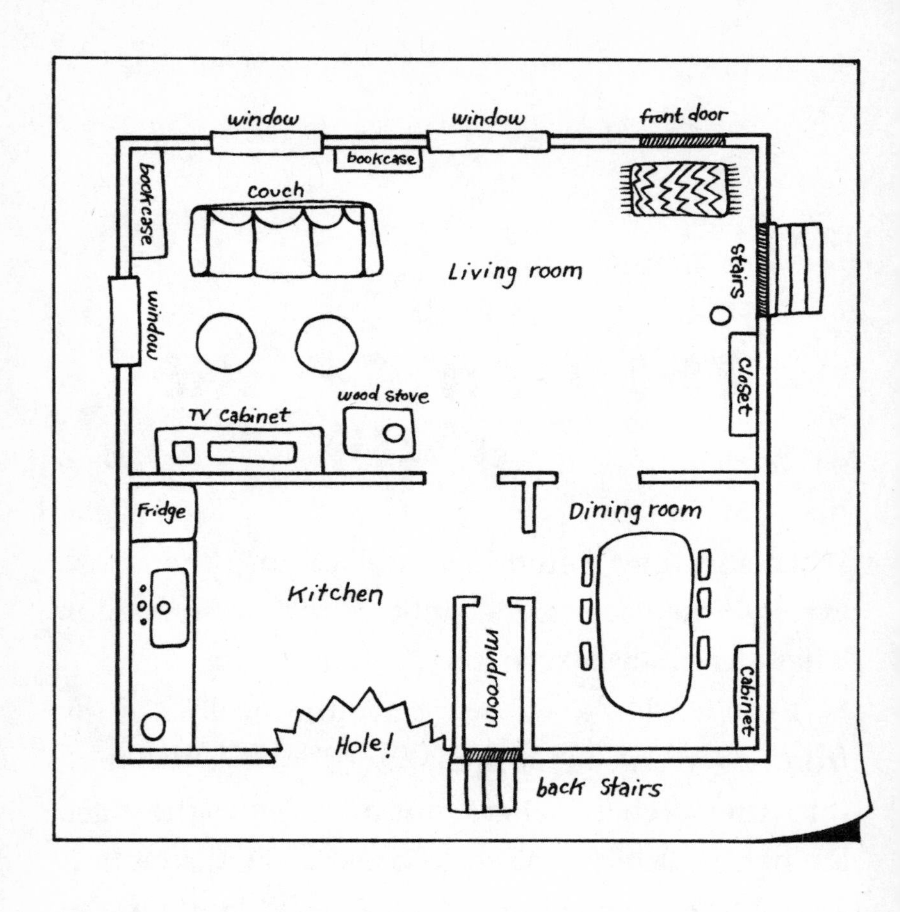

"Where's Grandma's stove?" asked Jessie.

"Well, *duh,*" said Evan, a little more sharply than he'd meant to. "They had to get rid of it. It was probably melted down to nothing."

"I thought you said it was a little fire," said Jessie.

"I thought it was," said Mrs. Treski.

"And why's it so cold?"

"I guess the heat isn't working?" answered their mom. "I didn't realize . . ."

Evan had never seen his mom so surprised. Usually, she handled just about anything that came her way: bats in the basement, a squirrel trapped in the chimney flue, the time that Jessie got her head stuck between the railings on the stairs. No matter what, you could count on their mom to solve pretty much any problem. But now she just stared at the hole in the wall and didn't move.

Evan reached under the sink and found the heavy Maglite that Grandma always kept there. He flashed the beam across the walls, looking for something—*anything*—that looked the way it was supposed to.

"What's that?" asked Jessie. Evan shone the flashlight where Jessie was pointing.

"Wow," said Evan.

"That's a hole," said Mrs. Treski. There was a two-foot-wide hole that went straight through the kitchen ceiling, which meant there was a hole in the floor upstairs. "What room are we under?"

Evan thought about how the rooms upstairs were laid out, but it was hard to piece it together. Was it Grandma's bedroom? Or Mom's old room? Jessie came up with the answer first. She was good with maps.

"It's Evan's room."

Oh, great, thought Evan.

All three of them trooped upstairs, Evan leading the way with the flashlight. Sure enough, all the doors to the upstairs rooms were open except for the one that led to Grandma's office, which doubled as Evan's bedroom when he visited. That door was shut tight with a layer of thick plastic taped over it. When they pushed it open, they found the hole in the floor. Both windows were shattered, the glass lying in shards scattered across the room. Again, someone had taped plastic around the edges, but the wind had teased its way in. When it blew outside, handfuls of snow gusted into the room and landed on the floor.

"You can't sleep in here, Evan," said his mom. "I

don't even want the two of you coming into this room at all. I'll clean up the glass tomorrow."

"Where am I going to sleep?" Evan asked. Ever since he was out of a crib, this had been his room at Grandma's house. He couldn't imagine sleeping anywhere else.

"Well, for tonight, why don't you sleep in Grandma's room?"

"No way," said Evan. There was something just not right about sleeping in his grandmother's bed. It was hers. "I'll sleep on the couch in the living room."

"Okay. It's probably going to be the warmest room in the house." The living room had a wood-burning stove that heated the whole downstairs. "I'll get the fire going, while you two unpack the car. Is it a plan?"

That sounded like the mother Evan was used to. He headed back out into the dark yard to start hauling in the suitcases and bags of groceries.

"This is weird," said Jessie, grabbing the handle of the biggest suitcase in the car.

"You can't carry that," said Evan. His sister was small for her age and weighed less than fifty pounds, but for some reason she always thought she could lift heavy stuff. "Let me do it. You take that one." He threw his weight into pulling the suitcase out of the trunk. It landed on the ground with a loud *ca-thunk.* "What's weird?" he asked.

"Everything," said Jessie. "Nothing is the way it's supposed to be."

"Well, relax. Grandma will be here tomorrow, and Mom said she already hired some guy to fix the wall. Anyway, we're not staying long. Maybe just three days. And it's still Grandma's house. How weird can it be?" But he knew exactly what Jessie meant.

Evan dragged the suitcase into the house, then walked back out to the car to get the food. Three days of sleeping on the couch. Three days with no room of his own. Three days without his friends.

Evan couldn't wait to go home.

As he pulled the last grocery bag out of the back seat, Evan heard a car coming up the long driveway. Night had fallen. Evan felt a moment of panic, the sudden feeling that he should protect the house and his mother and sister from whatever was coming toward them. For a second, he thought about running inside and locking the door, but then he remembered the hole in the kitchen wall. There was no way to keep an intruder out. Headlights rounded the bend and flashed on the house. Evan decided to stand his ground.

A gray pickup truck rattled to a stop right behind the Treskis' car, and a man stepped out. He was tall and rail thin, with a scraggly, pointy beard. He was wearing a long-sleeve T-shirt under a down vest, jeans, and heavy work boots, and he had a pair of headphones dangling loosely around his neck.

"Hey," said the man. "Is your mom around?"

Evan stood there looking at the man, trying to figure him out. Was he dangerous? Who was he?

The man stopped walking and stood in front of Evan. Then he stuck his hand out. "I'm Pete. I'm the one doing the work on your grandma's house."

Evan relaxed and shook Pete's hand. Up close, he could see that the guy wasn't that old. He looked about the same age as Adam's brother who was in college.

"So, is your mom around, or did you drive here by yourself?"

Evan smiled. "Yeah, right," he said. "She's inside. Mom! Mom!" He ran into the house and found his mother in the living room, closing the little door of the wood stove. A fire burned brightly inside, but the house was still as cold as a skating rink.

Pete introduced himself to Mrs. Treski and then went down to the basement to turn the electricity on. When he came back up, he walked her through the damage. The sink in the kitchen didn't have running water, and the electricity on the first floor had been knocked out. "I rigged up a couple of bypasses, but you're going to have to get a plumber and an electrician to do the real repair work," said Pete. "It's going to take a few weeks, maybe a month, before the house is really whole again. Are you staying here tonight?"

Mrs. Treski nodded.

"It'll be cold," said Pete, "even with the stove." He turned to Evan. "You need to keep that fire going all night. Can you do that?"

Evan straightened up. He'd been following Pete and his mother through the whole house, fascinated by the things that Pete described—the inner workings of the house, like it was an animal that lived and breathed. "Yeah," he said. "I know how to take care of a fire. I've been to sleep-away camp."

"Good," said Pete. "That's your job, then." He turned back to Mrs. Treski. "Do you want me to bring over a couple of space heaters for upstairs? I live just a mile up the road." But Mrs. Treski said no thanks, they'd be fine with the stove.

"Probably for the best," he said, nodding. "You'd blow a fuse for sure."

Evan followed Pete out to his truck, even though the snow was coming down harder now. Before climbing in, Pete said, "Are you the man of the family?"

Evan shrugged. "I guess so." His mom didn't really go for that "man of the family" thing. And even though Evan's dad had been gone for more than two years, Evan still didn't think of himself that way. He tried to help his mom as much as he could, but he was only ten.

"Okay, then," said Pete. "You'll help me tomorrow. Right?"

"Sure," said Evan. And all of a sudden, he wasn't so desperate to leave Grandma's house and go back home.

Chapter 3

You Don't See That Every Day

The plan had been to go get Grandma in the morning. She was getting discharged from the hospital first thing, which meant she could finally come home. Mrs. Treski decided they would stay through New Year's Day to make sure Grandma was settled. Jessie couldn't wait for Grandma to walk in the door. Maybe then things would go back to normal.

But the plan had to change, thanks to the storm. Overnight the snow had turned the whole world into a scene from the book that Jessie was reading—*The Lion, the Witch and the Wardrobe*—all winter white and silent. The driveway had disappeared under the heavy, fresh snow, and the local news reported that road conditions were "challenging." On top of that, the battery in the car was dead (because Jessie had left one of the interior lights on overnight), and it was going to be a while before the guy from AAA could come out to the house. Apparently, a lot of people were having car trouble because of the weather.

Jessie spent part of the morning curled up in front of the wood stove reading her book and eating from the box of store-bought powdered doughnuts that Pete had brought with him. Pete and Evan were down in the basement now, checking out the furnace. There was a lot of banging, and every once in a while she heard them laughing. Jessie didn't get it. What was so funny about a broken furnace?

After that, Jessie climbed the stairs to see what her mother was doing. She found Mrs. Treski in the room with the hole in the floor, going through boxes of papers that had gotten wet after the fire. She was looking for Grandma's homeowner's insurance policy. The woven rug with swirls of maroon and deepest blue was pulled back and folded over on itself, revealing the bare wooden floor beneath it.

"Ruined," said Mrs. Treski, as she worked her way through the box. "I don't think any of this can be saved." But she kept plucking through the papers.

Jessie started to wander over to the built-in bookcase that ran along one wall of the room. Grandma had bookcases in every room in the house, each one stuffed to overflowing, but the books in her office were the ones that were most important to her.

"Jessie, stop," said Mrs. Treski. "I'm not sure I got all the glass off the floor."

"I'm wearing shoes. I'll be careful," said Jessie, walking delicately across the floor. "Are Grandma's books ruined, too?"

"Some, probably. I hope not her favorites."

"They're all her favorites," said Jessie, staring at the bookcase.

These books were like old friends to Jessie. She'd known them since she was old enough to crawl into her grandmother's lap and sit patiently while Grandma turned the pages. Books on birds, books on meditation, books on string instruments and baseball and antique quilts. Aesop's fables and Greek mythology. She looked quickly for her favorite and found it exactly where she had left it the last time she visited.

It was called *The Big Book of Bells,* and it was more than one hundred years old. Jessie loved this book for a lot of reasons: the red tooled leather cover with gold lettering on the spine, the thick pages that made a whispery sound when you turned them, the photographs of men in bowler hats and ladies in long skirts. But mostly Jessie loved this book because it had a photograph of Grandma's bell in it, the very same bell that hung on Lovell's Hill.

Jessie tipped the book off the shelf and into her hand, relieved to see that it wasn't wet or burned. She carried it downstairs, settled herself on the couch, and turned first to the photo of Grandma's bell, feeling proud that it was so famous and important that it appeared in a book. Then she turned to the diagram that showed all the different parts of a bell.

The parts were named for parts of the human body, and most of them went in the order you would expect: the crown, the shoulder, the waist, the hip. But then came the lip! That always made Jessie laugh, to think of having lips on your hips.

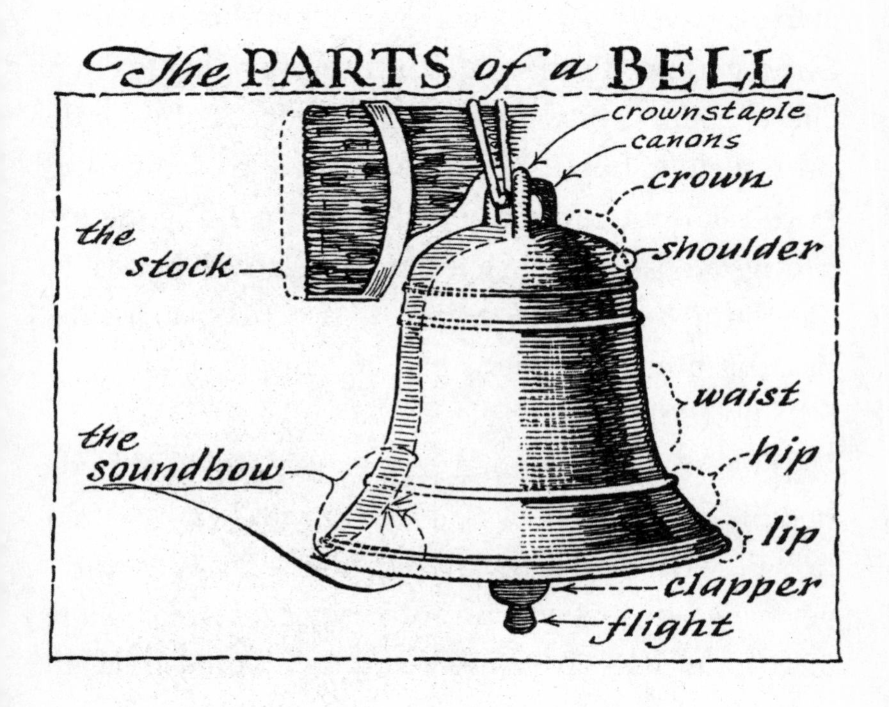

She was still poring over the book two hours later, reading about the largest bell in the world, which was in Russia, when the guy from AAA showed up and told Mrs. Treski that she needed an entirely new battery—which he didn't have on his truck. She would have to wait until later this afternoon when he could come back.

"No, no!" said Mrs. Treski. "You don't understand. I have to go pick up my mother this morning. She's getting discharged from the hospital." Then she explained how her mother had put the kettle on the stove but accidentally turned on the wrong burner and then forgotten all about it and gone for a long walk, and when she came back from her walk, she found her house on fire and tried to rush inside, but the fire department blocked her way, and she fell and broke her wrist.

The AAA guy listened very quietly and even nodded his head as if he was agreeing with her, but then he said what he'd already said. "I'm sorry, but I can't get back out this way until the afternoon. Probably after four." Mrs. Treski threw up her hands and said something under her breath, then she went back upstairs to continue sorting through Grandma's papers.

Jessie closed the book and went in the kitchen to try to convince Evan to go play in the snow with her. Evan was so wrapped up in helping Pete—they were tearing out the old wood from the wall—that she could hardly get him to even listen to her.

When Mrs. Treski finally drove off in the Subaru to get Grandma at the hospital, the afternoon sun was just beginning to draw long shadows on the blue-white snow. Jessie decided it was time to go visit Grandma's bell on the hill. She strapped a pair of snowshoes on her feet and headed outside.

The woods around the house were magical in any season, but especially in the wintertime. Two feet of fresh snow had fallen overnight. Jessie tried to imagine Mr. Tumnus, the faun in *The Lion, the Witch and the Wardrobe,* peeking out from behind a tree, his slender umbrella held in his hand. She wondered how fauns balanced on their two goat feet. It must be hard! She was pretty sure she would fall over, if she were half-human, half-goat.

She had reached the edge of the first woods and had come out into the clearing that was at the foot of a small hill. If she climbed over this hill and the next, she would come to Lovell's Hill with the bell at the top. But first she wanted to see if the tepee was still standing.

The summer before last, Jessie and Evan had built a tepee deep in the woods. First, they had found a dead tree trunk that stood about ten feet tall with all of its branches rotted away. Then they scoured the ground for deadwood branches that were at least eight feet long and mostly straight. Evan hauled the heavy branches back to the tree trunk. Sometimes he had to drag them a quarter of a mile over the bumpy floor of the woods. It was Jessie's job to snap off the spindly twigs that grew off the dead branches so that they were as straight and smooth as poles.

When they had a dozen straight branches, Evan and Jessie leaned them up against the trunk of the tree so that they made a circle all the way around. They covered the poles with fresh pine branches, using the stiff twine that Grandma kept in the barn to lash the branches to the poles. Over the opening, they hung a waterproof tarp that could be pulled aside like a door.

Before they had started building, Evan had made a diagram of the tepee. Jessie still had that drawing hanging on her bedroom wall back home.

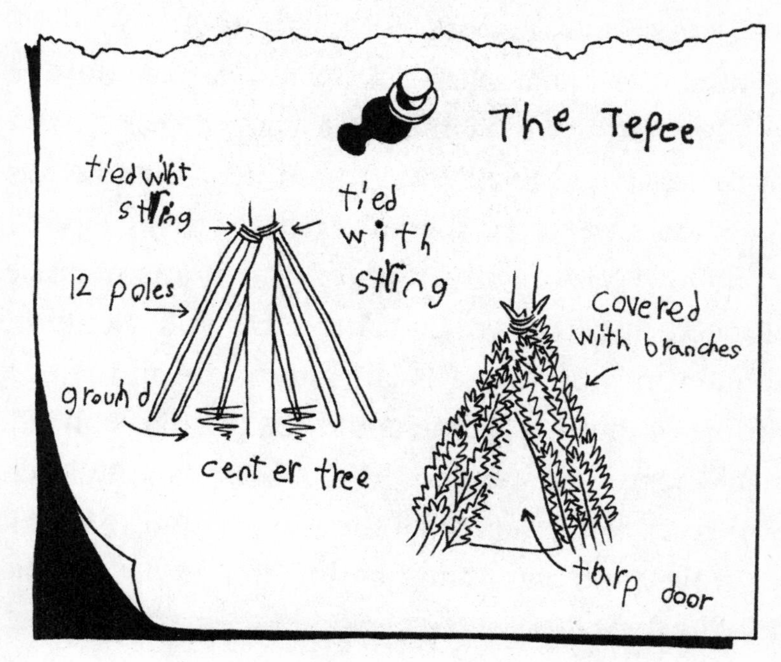

It took them two whole weeks to finish the tepee, but when they were done, they brought Grandma to see it and told her she could use it anytime she wanted. Evan had said, "This tepee will last a hundred years," and Grandma had agreed. Since then, she told Jessie that she often checked in on the tepee when she was out walking in the woods, just to make sure it was still in good shape. It was a nice place to rest, she said.

Jessie skirted the foot of the hills until she found the Lightning Tree that marked the way. Years ago the tree had been struck by lightning, leaving it scarred and black. Jessie and Evan always used it as a marker; its one remaining stub of a branch pointed to the tepee.

Following the direction of the branch, Jessie plunged into the woods. There was still plenty of light, even though it was late afternoon, and after a couple of minutes, Jessie could see the tepee ahead, just where it was supposed to be. She snowshoed over to it, walked once all the way around to check for holes, and then climbed inside and sat on the dry dirt floor.

Jessie loved the tepee. It made her feel safe and warm and hidden away from the world. She lay on her back and stared up at the branches over her head. *This will never change,* she thought with satisfaction. She stayed inside for a few minutes, then crawled out of the tepee and snowshoed back to the foot of the first small hill.

But when she began to climb the hill, she saw that she wasn't alone. A boy was cross-country skiing toward her, his head down, goggles strapped to his face. It took Jessie a minute to realize that the boy didn't see her. He was headed straight for her, and he was picking up speed as he came down the hill.

"Hey!" she shouted. She lifted her big floppy snowshoes awkwardly and tried to back up into the woods. But the tail of one of the shoes stepped on the tail of the other one, and she ended up falling over backwards. "Hey!" she shouted again, as the boy *shooshed* straight toward her.

"Whoa!" he said, sliding to a snowplow stop. "You don't see that every day."

"What?" asked Jessie.

"My name's Maxwell. Who are you?" He made a funny move, shuffling his right foot forward and leaning his weight on it, and then stepping back onto his left. It almost looked like a dance move, except that he was on skis.

"I'm Jessie. You practically ran me over!"

"But I didn't!" he said, doing the dance move again. "That's 'cause I'm smart!" He made a funny noise that was like a steam engine puffing on a track.

"I wouldn't exactly call it smart," said Jessie, struggling to her feet. "But at least you didn't kill me."

She snowshoed her way past Maxwell and started to trudge up the hill that he'd just skied down.

"Where are you going?"

"That way," said Jessie, pointing up the hill.

"Can I come?"

"I don't care," said Jessie. She didn't say it angrily. It was just the honest truth.

Jessie noticed that Maxwell liked to talk. A lot.

On the way up the hill, she learned that Maxwell lived in the house closest to Grandma's and that his family had just moved in before the school year started. He spent a lot of time at Grandma's house. In fact, it had been Maxwell who discovered the house on fire after Grandma had left her stove on and then gone out for a walk. He'd run home to tell his mother, and she was the one who called the fire department.

"You don't see that every day!" said Maxwell, after describing what the fire had looked like.

Jessie looked at him. There was something funny about this kid.

They had crossed the first hill and the second, and now they were at the bottom of Lovell's Hill, the highest of the little hills on this part of Grandma's property. In five minutes Jessie would reach the top and be able to see the wooden crossbeam and the bell. The crossbeam was made out of two heavy oak beams that were joined in the shape of an upside-down L. When Jessie was younger, she would ask Evan to lift her up so that she could hang on the end of the top beam and swing her legs back and forth, pretending that she was a second bell, ringing. Now that she was older, the crossbeam was only a little taller than she was, so she didn't need anyone to lift her up.

Jessie trudged forward, Maxwell gliding alongside. She was almost there. She could just see the top of the crossbeam. The afternoon sun was starting to set, slicing its way down Black Bear Mountain. It was hard to look up at the crest of the hill, because the sun was setting directly behind it, causing the snow to glint fiercely. Jessie shielded her eyes and tried to see the top of the hill. Maxwell was *shooshing* by her side, swinging his poles back and forth with wild flailing motions, cutting new tracks in the untouched snow.

Trudge, trudge, trudge. Jessie looked up once more just as the sun dipped below the mountain, throwing the hillside into sudden shadow. There was the crest. There was the wooden crossbeam.

But the bell was gone.

Chapter 4
That Bad Feeling

Evan stared in amazement. The hole in the wall was gone. He and Pete had worked all day, first ripping out the damaged studs and replacing them with clean, dry wood, then trimming the old boards so that the ragged hole became a neat rectangle, then measuring and cutting and nailing in the new sheets of plywood. There was still the dry wall to hang and the outside shingles to replace, but the hole was gone. Evan had never felt such a sense of accomplishment in his life, not even when he and Jessie had won the Labor Day Poster Contest at the end of the summer.

Now he was sweeping up the sawdust that lay as thick as a carpet under his feet. Pete said no carpenter worth his salt leaves a mess behind at the end of the day. So Evan was sweeping up the saw-dust and bent nails and small chips of wood, while Pete hauled the bigger scraps out to the truck. But every once in a while, Evan stopped and held the broom still in his hands so that he could admire the work they had done. He couldn't wait to show his mom when she got back from the hospital.

He was dumping the last pile of sawdust into the large gray plastic barrel when he heard loud clomp-ing on the front porch, followed by the front door opening. Evan walked into the living room just as Jessie tried to step over the threshold wearing her snowshoes.

"Evan! The bell is gone!" She tripped over the doormat and fell face first into the living room, land-ing hard on her hands and knees. Behind her was an older boy Evan had never seen before. He had funny-looking cross-country shoe-boots on his feet, and he was carrying a pair of ski poles. Evan guessed he was at least twelve, maybe thirteen.

"I can't get these off," said Jessie. She had rolled onto her back in the living room and was holding her feet up in the air. The snowshoes were dripping clumps of snow onto her face and the floor. "Help me, Evan!"

"Oh, for Pete's sake," he said. He crossed over to where she was squirming and grabbed hold of one of the snowshoes. The boy had a funny smile on his face and was rocking back and forth, one foot out in front of the other. "Hey," said Evan, as a way of introducing himself.

"You don't see that every day," said the boy, looking at Jessie, who looked like a ladybug caught on her back.

"Yeah, actually, I do," said Evan. Jessie was always tripping over something or getting caught on something or dragging something along behind her. Evan unclipped one snowshoe and then the other and flipped them off Jessie's feet.

"The bell is gone, Evan! Gone!"

"What do you mean? Grandma's bell?"

"Yes! The New Year's Eve bell!"

"It can't be gone. You must have climbed the wrong hill."

"No, we didn't. The wooden post was there, just like always, but the bell is gone!"

Evan shook his head. "That thing weighs—I don't know—a hundred pounds. There's no way someone could just walk off with it. And besides, who would want to take it?"

"Who *wouldn't* want to take it?" Jessie asked, bouncing from one foot to the other. "It's an antique and it's famous—"

"It's not famous, Jessie," said Evan, shaking his head. "Just 'cause it's in that book doesn't make it famous."

"Well, it's worth two thousand five hundred dollars!"

"Is not!"

"I'll show you!" Jessie ran to the couch where she'd left *The Big Book of Bells* that morning and pulled out a letter that was tucked into the back cover of the book. She handed it to Evan, who read it slowly, not understanding all the words but getting the general idea. About five years ago, Grandma had had the bell appraised to find out how much it was worth, and Jessie was right: the letter said the bell was worth $2,500.

"Wow," said Evan.

Maxwell bobbed his head several times, rocking back and forth on his feet.

"We've got to find it," said Jessie, pulling on Evan's arm. "New Year's Eve is in three days! If we don't ring the bell on New Year's Eve . . ." Jessie couldn't get the words out, and Evan knew what she was feeling. It was hard to imagine not ringing the bell on New Year's Eve. They had always done that, for as long as he could remember.

Evan looked at the boy and then back at his sister. "Jessie . . . ?" He half pointed at Maxwell, hoping his sister would get the hint, but as usual, she didn't. "Uh, my name's Evan," he said to the boy, sticking out his hand the way grownups did.

"How do you do," said the boy, shaking Evan's hand. "My name's Maxwell. I'm smart!" Then he rocked forward on his left foot and shook his right hand in the air. Evan looked at him closely.

"Maxwell lives in the yellow house. The one with

the big rock out front," said Jessie. "He knows Grandma really well."

"Yep," said Maxwell. "I come here all the time." Maxwell was rocking back and forth steadily now, snapping his right hand in the air with each forward motion. "We watch TV. And we do puzzles. And we feed the birds. And I'm smart! That's what Mrs. Joyce says. She says, 'Maxwell, you are smart!' "

There was a moment's silence, and then Evan asked, "What grade are you in?"

"Sixth grade," said Maxwell. "Hardy Middle School. Grade six."

"Mom's home!" shouted Jessie, running for the front door. Evan had heard it, too—the old Subaru making its way up the long driveway. He hurried back into the kitchen. He wanted to get the trash barrel outside before his mom walked in.

He was carrying it down the makeshift back steps he and Pete had rigged up, when Pete came around the house. "Your grandma's home, so I'm heading out for the day," said Pete. "We'll hang the dry wall tomorrow, then we'll start on the upstairs the next day. Sound good?"

"Yeah, sure," said Evan. He wanted to sound casual about it, so Pete wouldn't think this was the first construction job he'd ever done, but he couldn't keep the eagerness out of his voice.

"Okay, then. See you tomorrow." Pete plugged in his headphones and headed for his truck.

Evan walked back into the kitchen and took one more look around. It was still definitely a disaster area, but they'd accomplished a lot: the wall was repaired, and the back door was framed and hung, and you could walk up and down the back steps if you were careful. Plus, it was a whole lot cleaner than it had been an hour ago. When Evan heard voices (mostly Jessie's) in the living room, he hurried in to say hello.

His grandmother stood just inside the doorway, next to the coat rack and umbrella stand. Her winter parka was draped over her shoulders as if it were a cape, and Evan could see that her arm was in a cast, cradled in a sling around her neck. She fumbled one-handed with the coat until Evan's mother took it from her and hung it up on the rack.

Evan watched as Jessie tried to grab hold of

Grandma's hand, but Grandma pulled her hand in, hunching forward protectively, and covered the sling with her good arm, as if she were afraid someone might try to steal something away from her. She began to walk toward the middle of the room, taking small steps, which was not at all the way his grandmother usually walked. Then she stopped and looked at the stairs that led to the second floor and then back at the front door.

It was her face that surprised Evan the most. It looked pale, and she had bags under her eyes, which Evan had never noticed before. Most of all, she couldn't seem to settle her gaze on anything. Her eyes kept flitting around the room, like a bird that won't perch on any one thing.

Jessie was hopping around like a bird, too, chattering nonstop about the bell. Maxwell was walking behind them, carrying on his own conversation and making a strange puffing noise that sounded like he was trying to blow feathers out of his mouth. Evan's mother had an arm around his grandma's shoulder, guiding her slowly toward the couch, and when

Evan caught sight of his mother's face, he knew right away that something was very wrong.

"Hi, Grandma," said Evan cheerfully, from across the room. But Grandma didn't look at him.

"She's tired," said his mom. "Jessie, would you please stop asking so many questions. Grandma needs a couple of minutes to get used to being home."

"Why?" asked Jessie. "Why do you need to get used to being home, Grandma? That doesn't make any sense."

"Jessie, shut it," said Evan, feeling a little panicked. What he really wanted to do was run up to his mother and get a hug from her, but with Maxwell standing right there, there was no way he was going to do that.

"Come see the kitchen, Grandma," said Jessie. "See how good it looks."

"Jessie," warned her mother, "you need to slow down."

"A cup of tea," said Grandma. "That's what I need. A good strong cup of green tea."

She started to walk toward the kitchen. Evan hurried ahead of her, scooping up two last stray nails that were on the Formica counter. Then he stood beside the patched hole. His mother and grandmother walked into the kitchen, trailed by Jessie and Maxwell, who had finally stopped talking. Everyone looked at Evan and the repair work that he and Pete had done that day. It was his grandmother who spoke first.

"What is this? What has happened here?"

"Mom," said Mrs. Treski. "There was a fire. Do you remember the fire?"

"Where's my stove? How am I going to make my tea without a stove?"

"The stove was ruined, Grandma," said Jessie. "They had to take it out because it was no good anymore."

"What do you mean, Jessie?" asked Grandma. "Who did this? Where was I?" She looked at Mrs. Treski. "Susan, what has been going on here?"

"Mom—"

"You don't see that every day!" said Maxwell, rocking back and forth nervously. His right hand snapped in the air like he was cracking the whip on an imaginary horse.

"No, you certainly don't, Maxwell," said Evan's grandma. "You certainly don't."

"Grandma," said Evan. "It's going to be okay. Me and Pete are fixing the whole thing. We're going to work some more tomorrow. We'll get it just the way it used to be." Evan could feel that bad feeling rising up in him. The feeling he got just before taking a test. The feeling he sometimes got late at night when the house was too quiet and too dark and he wished his dad had never left.

For the first time that afternoon, Evan's grandmother looked right at him. She peered sharply at his face and then looked him over once, from top to bottom. She turned to Evan's mom.

"Who is that boy?" she asked angrily. "Did he do this to my kitchen?"

"Mom," said Mrs. Treski. "It's Evan. Your grandson."

Evan's grandmother shook her head. "I don't know him. Make him go away."

Chapter 5
A Thousand Pieces

The next morning, Jessie sat with her grandmother at the dining room table and ripped the cellophane wrapper off the box of the new jigsaw puzzle. She couldn't wait to get started. Grandma looked like herself this morning. She had slept twelve hours last night, and at breakfast she'd given Jessie and Evan a giant bear hug. They'd even exchanged their Christmas gifts. Grandma was wearing the scarf that Jessie had knit for her draped over her shoulders, and Jessie had a brand-new calligraphy pen and two jars of metallic ink waiting for her upstairs in her room. Evan's present from Grandma was a magic set, and he had given her a Christmas cactus covered in pink blossoms.

"That looks good enough to eat," said Grandma, staring at the picture of the puzzle that Jessie set up on one end of the table like a billboard. The brightly colored jellybeans reminded Jessie of Christmas lights all in a tangled pile. They even seemed to glisten and glow like lights on a tree. It was the most beautiful puzzle she had ever seen.

And the hardest. It took Jessie and Grandma nearly ten minutes just to spread out all the pieces on the table and turn each one right side up. Then they had to separate out all the straight-edge pieces that would form the outside frame. When they had finished, they stopped and studied the puzzle.

"They all look the same," said Jessie. It was true. Even though the pieces were different shapes, the picture on each one was basically the same. There was no way to pick one out from all the others. Jessie had never done a puzzle like this before. She didn't know where to begin.

"Four corners," said Grandma, tapping the table. "That's how we always start, right?"

So they searched through the puzzle pieces until

they found the four corner pieces and matched those up to the picture to figure out which corner went where. Then they began the slow process of building off the corners to create the outside frame of the puzzle.

"Grandma, tell me about the New Year's Eve bell," said Jessie. She'd been waiting all morning to ask her grandmother about the bell, but she was nervous. Mrs. Treski had warned both children: "Try not to say anything that might upset her," and she had told Jessie specifically, "Don't talk about how the bell is missing."

"Well, what do you want to know?" asked Grandma, fitting a puzzle piece onto her side of the frame.

"Where did it come from?"

"My great-grandfather put it there to call the neighbors in case of an emergency."

"Like what?" asked Jessie. "What kind of emergency?" She was hunting for a straight-edge piece with a purple jellybean on it.

"Oh, all kinds of things. If someone was sick or

if there was a lost child or a fire or a pack of wolves getting into the sheep."

"Back in 1884?" Over the years, Jessie had traced her fingers over that date on the bell a hundred times. She knew the inscription by heart:

THE JONES TROY BELL
FOUNDRY COMPANY,
TROY, N.Y. 1884.
I SOUND THE ALARM
TO KEEP THE PEACE.

The letters were as tall as her thumb.

"That's when the bell was cast." Jessie's grandma nodded. "That's when the bell was hung."

"How did they hang it?" asked Jessie. "It must weigh a thousand pounds!"

"Oh, no," said Grandma, scratching her earlobe, which is what she did when she concentrated. "It doesn't weigh that much. Maybe a hundred pounds. Two men could hang that bell easily. One time, years and years ago, the bell needed to be cleaned, so I lifted it off the hooks and dragged it back to the house on a sledge all by myself. Of course, it's a lot easier to take a bell down than it is to hang it up."

"You took the bell down?" asked Jessie. "When?"

"Oh, years ago. A long time ago. Just after your grandfather died. I was still young and strong back then. Not like now." Grandma turned a puzzle piece around in her hand, seeing if it would fit, but then put it back with the others on the table.

"Grandma?" Jessie asked in a near whisper. "Did you take the bell down—sometime this year?"

Grandma laughed. "What a thing! No, I couldn't take that bell down anymore. That old bell is still up there on Lovell's Hill. Always will be." She had stopped working on the puzzle and was using her good hand to rub her shoulder as if it ached.

"Maybe you wanted to sell it?" asked Jessie, thinking of the appraisal letter.

"No, Jessie. I would never sell the New Year's Eve bell."

"Maybe you . . . forgot."

"I didn't forget, Jessie," said Grandma, shaking her head.

"But you could have—"

"No!" Her grandmother dropped her hand to the table so that it made a sharp rapping sound. "Now stop, Jessie! The bell is on the hill. It's always been there, and it always will be there. So, enough."

"Okay, Grandma," said Jessie, but inside she wondered if maybe her grandmother's forgetfulness was a clue to the mystery of the missing bell.

They worked on the puzzle for another minute in silence, and then Jessie heard a strange thud on the front door. When she got up to investigate, she found Maxwell standing in front of the house with skis on his feet and ski poles in one hand. In his other hand, he had a snowball, and Jessie noticed the *splot* of white on the front door where he had already thrown one.

"You're home," said Maxwell.

"Uh-huh," said Jessie. They stared at each other for a minute, Maxwell rocking back and forth on his skis, Jessie with her arms crossed in front of her.

"It's not polite to ask someone to invite you in," said Maxwell.

"Why not?" asked Jessie.

"I don't know," said Maxwell. "It's just a rule my mother taught me."

"It doesn't make sense," said Jessie. "How's the person supposed to know you want to get invited in if you don't ask?" She wondered why they were talking about this. It was a strange topic for Maxwell to bring up out of the blue.

Maxwell nodded his head. "But it's a rule," he said.

"Maxwell!" Jessie's grandma had come to the open door. "Do you want to come inside?"

"Uh-huh!" he said, using his pole to unsnap his boots from his skis. Jessie followed her grandma back into the house with Maxwell right behind.

"It's a good thing you're here," said Grandma. "I need to go lie down for a few minutes, and Jessie needs a puzzle partner. Want to take over?" she asked, pointing to the dining room table.

Maxwell didn't even answer. He just walked over to the table and sat down in the chair that Grandma had left empty.

"Prepare to be amazed," Grandma said to Jessie, and then she headed up the stairs.

When Jessie sat in her seat, Maxwell had already fit together three pieces. But they weren't pieces of the outside frame of the puzzle. They were pieces that belonged in the vast, empty middle—the part of the puzzle Jessie hadn't even tried to solve yet.

And he kept finding more. He fit another piece onto the three he'd already joined. And then another. His eyes roamed quickly over the pieces, and he moved his hands over them, too, his fingers snapping and wiggling as he thought about which piece to pick up next. Sometimes he made a mistake—a near miss—but just as often he got the right piece on the first try. *Snap.* The piece fit in perfectly, and then Maxwell started to look for the next one.

"How do you do that?" asked Jessie. She was really good at jigsaw puzzles, the best in the family, the best of anyone she knew. But she couldn't start *in the middle* of a thousand-piece puzzle, especially one that was a picture of nothing but jellybeans.

"I'm smart," said Maxwell, continuing to add pieces. *Snap. Snap.*

"Well, I'm smart, too, but I can't do that," she said. She tried to concentrate on the frame she was building, but Maxwell's movements were so annoying, she couldn't keep her mind on what she was doing.

"Jellybeans," said Maxwell, snapping his fingers and looking at the pieces.

"Yeah, jellybeans," said Jessie, absent-mindedly. "Grandma calls me Jessie Bean."

"Why?" asked Maxwell.

"It's a nickname."

"I hate nicknames," Maxwell said loudly. "Nick-names are mean."

Jessie looked up, surprised. She'd always thought the same thing but had never heard anyone say it before. "Yeah, I hate nicknames, too! I wish everyone would just call people by their real names. Right?"

"Right," said Maxwell, snapping another piece in place. He pointed at the cluster of puzzle pieces he had fit together. "You don't see that every day."

"What?" asked Jessie, looking at the pieces.

"Oklahoma," said Maxwell. And sure enough, Jessie could see that the pieces made a shape that looked like Oklahoma.

Jessie watched as Maxwell added piece after piece to the puzzle. She was starting to get annoyed. At this rate, she wasn't going to get to do any of her own puzzle. "You know what?" she said. "I like to do puzzles all by myself, without any help." This wasn't true, but it was no fun doing a puzzle with someone who could finish the whole thing before you even got a corner done. It was like someone giving you the answer to a math problem before you even started. "Let's do something else. What do you want to do?"

"*Get Smart*!" said Maxwell.

"What?"

"The best TV show ever made. *Get Smart.* Six seasons, 1965 to 1970, one hundred and thirty-eight episodes produced in all." Maxwell walked over to the TV cabinet and opened the lower cupboard. Inside, Grandma had a few DVDs, mostly babyish movies that Jessie and Evan didn't watch anymore. But Maxwell pulled out a boxed set that Jessie had never seen before. *Get Smart* was the title, and there was a picture of a man in a suit and a tie looking very surprised.

"Season one, the pilot episode," said Maxwell. He popped the DVD in the player, and they both sat down on the couch to watch. The title of the first episode was "Mr. Big."

It was a funny show. Jessie laughed and laughed. There was this dopey secret agent who worked for a super-secret government agency called CONTROL. The agent's name was Maxwell Smart, but his code name was Agent 86.

"I get it," she said, turning to Maxwell. "That's why you say you're smart all the time. Maxwell Smart! It's a joke!"

Maxwell bobbed his head up and down. "Yep! My name is Maxwell, and I'm smart. That's what Mrs. Joyce always says! She says, 'You're smart, Maxwell.' It's a joke!"

Maxwell Smart was a no-nonsense secret agent.

He liked to take charge, and he was always confident he would catch the criminal in the end. Some people might think he was kind of bossy, but Jessie thought he was great.

There was another secret agent—a dark-haired woman named Agent 99—and a dog named K-13. Together, they got to use all kinds of great gadgets, like bino-specs and an inflato-coat and a shoe phone. Jessie especially loved the bino-specs.

"We should do that," she said at the end of the first episode. "We should be like spies and have a stakeout and figure out who stole the bell. We could solve the crime, just like Maxwell Smart and Agent 99."

"Okay," said Maxwell. "Let's do that."

"No, I mean for real," said Jessie. "Real secret agents, not just pretend."

"Okay," said Maxwell. "Let's do that."

"Really?" said Jessie. She was surprised that Maxwell agreed with her right away. She figured it would take a while to convince a sixth-grader to go

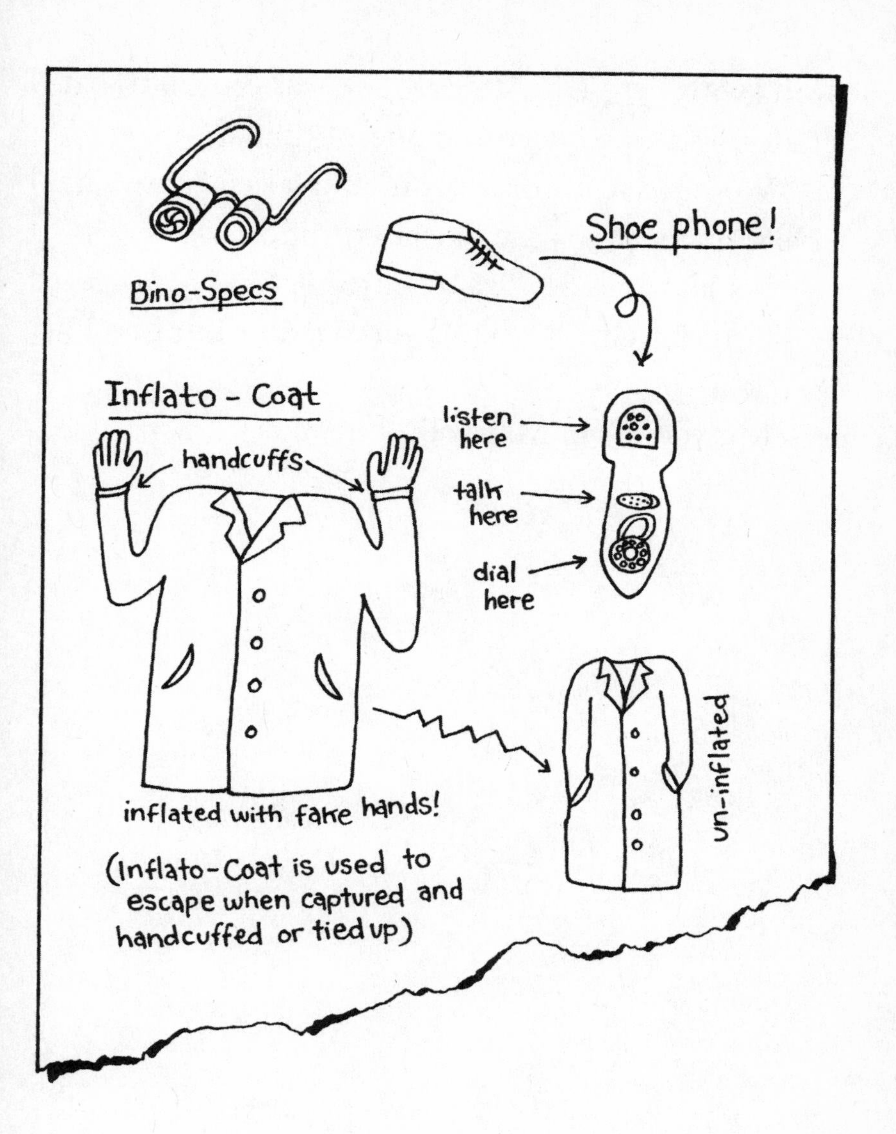
Bino-Specs
Shoe phone!
listen here
talk here
dial here
Inflato - Coat
handcuffs
inflated with fake hands!
(Inflato-Coat is used to escape when captured and handcuffed or tied up)
un-inflated

along with her plan. After all, she was only a fourth-grader, and a pretty young one, at that.

"We have to think of something fast," she said. "New Year's Eve is the day after tomorrow."

"It's like a puzzle," said Maxwell.

"You're right. It's like a puzzle, and I'm good at puzzles."

"Me, too," said Maxwell. "I'm smart."

Chapter 6
Afternoon Shadows

Evan didn't want to stop. He and Pete were fixing the holes in the roof. Pete was outside, up on the extension ladder, ripping up shingles and tossing them through the hole to Evan. Evan was inside, crouching under the sloping ceiling so that he could catch the shingles as they fell and heave them into the garbage barrel. He also had to hand Pete whatever tools he needed.

So when Mrs. Treski appeared in the doorway of Grandma's office/construction site and asked Evan if he would please take Grandma for a walk, he made a face and said, "Can't Jessie do it?"

Evan, kneeling under the hole, looked up and caught sight of Pete's face looking right back at him. Pete didn't need to say a word. He just shook his head once, and Evan knew that was that.

"Yeah, okay, Mom," said Evan. He stood up and wiped the grit from the knees of his pants. "I'll be back in a few minutes," he hollered up to Pete.

"I'll be here," Pete called down. "Same as before. Take good care of your grandma, Big E."

Evan followed his mother, scowling. "Why can't Grandma take a walk by herself?" Grandma was a nut about walking. She took long walks by herself every day. Sometimes she'd walk five miles, circling her property, which covered a hundred acres at the foot of Black Bear Mountain.

"Evan, please," said his mother in the voice she used that meant there would be no more discussion.

Evan walked into the mudroom just off the kitchen. Grandma was looping her new purple scarf around her neck, the one that Jessie had knit for her for Christmas. Her injured arm was tucked inside her bulky winter coat, which was zipped closed over it.

"Hey, Grandma," said Evan.

"Something tells me you don't feel like going for a walk right now," said Grandma. Evan bent over his boots, tugging them onto his feet and hiding his face. Was it that obvious? The memory of what his grandmother had said to him two days ago in the kitchen flickered in his brain, but then he remembered his mother's explanation. *She's not herself, Evan.*

"No, I want to go," he said, knowing that it was okay to fudge the truth when you didn't want to hurt someone's feelings. "It's just that I was helping Pete, and he kind of needs me right now."

"Pete's a good boy," said Grandma.

"Boy!" said Evan. "He's a grown man."

"Not to me, he's not. Everyone looks young to me!" Grandma used her mouth to hold a mitten still while she wriggled her good hand into it. "Ready?"

"Ready," said Evan. Grandma opened the back door and was just about to step out, when Evan's mother called from upstairs. Evan tromped up to the second floor, feeling hot and puffy in his heavy ski coat and boots.

"Evan," said his mother, "try to make it a short walk, okay? Grandma thinks she's back to her old self, but I don't want her getting too tired. And try to hold on to her good arm, if she'll let you. Or at least keep close to her, so if she trips you can grab her before she falls. Okay?"

Evan didn't like the sound of any of this, but he nodded his head. He wasn't used to taking care of his grandma. She had always taken such good care of him and Jessie.

"And, Evan, one more thing," said his mother. "Don't let her go near the bell. Okay? I don't want her . . . Just keep her away from that hill, okay?"

Afternoon shadows came early to Grandma's woods because the sun set behind the mountain. Evan was surprised that the blue-gray light of late afternoon was already painting the snow. He turned to walk up the long, plowed driveway toward the main road—that would be a good half-mile walk—

but Grandma said she wanted to walk a different way, through the woods. She set out on the path that headed for the foot of Black Bear Mountain. There were footprints in the snow along this path and the steady slicing marks of skis, so Evan knew that Jessie and Maxwell had already come this way today.

Evan talked about the repair work that he and Pete were doing, especially the thrilling part about ripping out the old scorched studs in the wall and putting in new ones. It had been tricky, because the wall they were working on was a load-bearing wall, which meant it was holding up a lot of the weight of the second story. If they took out too many studs at once, the whole house could collapse. Evan thought it was like playing Jenga—the game where you build a tower of blocks, then try to pull out each block without causing the tower to fall.

Grandma didn't say much. It took some effort to walk on the packed-down snow, and there were branches and rocks you had to watch out for. Even Evan could feel his heart beating fast with the effort, and the cold intake of each breath of frozen air made his breathing seem heavier. He thought about Pete up on the roof all afternoon and wondered how he did it.

"Grandma, you want to go back now?" The light was definitely fading, and they'd already been walking for fifteen minutes. Evan wasn't even quite sure where they were, but Grandma knew her property like the back of her hand.

Grandma shook her head but didn't say anything. Her breathing was louder now, and she was grunting a little with the effort of climbing uphill. It was a pretty big hill, and the snow seemed deeper here. Evan looked around. There was something familiar about this place, but the light was so soft and lavender that he couldn't really trust his eyes.

They were just reaching the top now, Grandma ahead of him by a few feet. And as the crest of the hill came into view, Evan felt a sudden sense of coldness and dread.

Usually, they came up this hill from the other side, but it was still the same hill. Lovell's Hill. The one with the bell. There was the wooden crossbeam. And just like Jessie had said, the bell was gone.

"Grandma! Let's go back now," said Evan, afraid but not sure of what—which just made the fear feel all the worse. But Grandma wasn't stopping. She made a beeline for the bell, or at least where the bell should have been. Evan felt as though he had never seen a space so empty as the place where the bell was supposed to hang.

When she reached the wooden crossbeam, Grandma stopped. She looked around, and then looked back at the empty space. In the dim light, Evan couldn't see her face very well, but what he saw frightened him. She didn't look like his grandmother. She looked strange, with one arm missing inside her coat and the empty, flopping sleeve hanging like a dead fish. Her knitted cap was crooked on her head, and one strand of gray hair hung down and curled around her neck. Her eyes were searching for something, but the dying light made it harder and harder to see. Evan looked around to try to understand what she was looking for, but the thick blanket of snow seemed to transform every rock, every tree, every shape into something else. It was hard to make sense of any of it.

"Did you take the bell?" asked his grandmother sharply.

"No!" said Evan.

"Where is it? What have you done with it?"

"I don't know, Grandma. I didn't do anything with it."

"Give it back. Right now. It isn't yours to take."

"I didn't take it," said Evan, his panic growing. He had to figure out some way to get Grandma home. But when he took a step toward her, she backed up and nearly fell over. Evan froze in his tracks.

"Who are you?" she asked angrily.

"Grandma, it's me. It's Evan."

"Thief. You're a bell thief." Grandma looked at the crossbeam again and then at the sky. Evan tried desperately to think of how he was going to get Grandma home. She was tired. She was cold. He could see that now. He had to figure out how to take care of her. But he couldn't think. Should he leave her here and go get help? Should he try to force her to go home? How was he going to get her to safety without hurting her?

"Grandma, it's me. Evan. I'm your grandson. I need to get you home, okay?" Again Evan took a step toward her, and this time Grandma did fall over backwards, trying to move away from him. She landed sitting down in the soft snow, her bad arm still tucked inside her coat. Evan didn't think she was hurt, but the fall seemed to frighten her even more. She looked at Evan as if he had pushed her down, even though he was standing ten feet away from her.

"Stay away!" she said. "You won't get away with this." She looked around her again, and said, "Where's Susan?"

Evan didn't know what to do. He didn't know what to say. The truth made no sense as long as Grandma didn't know who he was.

He tried to think. He tried to imagine what it must feel like to be his grandmother right now.

Finally, he said, "Susan sent me, Mrs. Joyce. She asked me to bring you home. She's waiting for you at home." Evan waited to see how she would respond.

"Good," said Grandma. "I need to speak with her. There's been a problem. A very big problem." But she didn't seem to remember what the problem was.

"Can I help you up?" asked Evan. He didn't move toward her.

"Yes. Help me up. Then take me to Susan. I need to speak with her."

Evan slowly walked over to his grandmother and helped lift her to her feet. It was hard to get her up, and he could feel his muscles straining, but he was able to do it.

"What's your name?" asked Grandma, straightening her cap on her head.

Suddenly, Evan recalled a character in a story that he and Jessie had made up when they were younger. "Grumpminster Fink. At your service, madam." He crooked out his arm.

"That's a very strange name," she said, but she took hold of his elbow, and slowly they made their way down off the hill, out of the woods, away from the falling night, and into the warmth and brightness of the house.

Chapter 7

Chickens

Jessie looked up from her notebook as Evan walked into the living room. She and Maxwell had spent most of the day walking all over Grandma's property, looking for someone to spy on. Now they were watching *Get Smart* while Jessie wrote important notes that would help them with their spy mission. They'd finished watching the episode called "Diplomat's Daughter" and were about to watch the one where Maxwell Smart disguises himself as a giant chicken. At the top of the first page of her notebook, Jessie had written, "The Bell Bandit," which she thought sounded just like the title of a real episode from the show.

When Evan walked in, Jessie was surprised to

see that he had his snow boots on. “Not allowed!” she said, pointing her pencil at the dripping boots. “You’re tracking in snow!”

“Mom!” shouted Evan. “Mom, can you come here?” Jessie looked at Evan’s face. It didn’t look the way it usually did. It almost looked like Evan was scared of something. But that didn’t make any sense, because there was nothing to be afraid of here in the house. Jessie looked over at Maxwell. He hadn’t even noticed that Evan had come in the room. He was busy watching the television.

“What is it?” shouted Mrs. Treski from the second floor.

Evan took the stairs two at a time. Ten seconds later, Mrs. Treski came hurrying down with Evan right behind her. Without saying a word, they disappeared into the kitchen. Jessie slowly got up from the couch and wandered after them, not sure she wanted to see what was going on.

In the kitchen, Jessie’s mom was trying to take Grandma’s coat off, but Grandma kept twisting away, saying it was time to feed the chickens.

Chickens! Just like on *Get Smart.* But Jessie knew that Grandma didn't keep chickens anymore. She used to, for years and years, and Jessie remembered the smelly coop and the soft fluff of feathers when she held a hen and the warm, smooth eggs that came in all different colors. That had been a long time ago, when Jessie was just a little kid. Why was Grandma saying she had to feed the chickens now?

"I'll feed the chickens, Mrs. Joyce," said Evan. Why was Evan calling Grandma *Mrs. Joyce*? "I'll take care of everything."

"You don't know how!" said Grandma angrily. "Susan, stop it. I have my chores to do." She swatted at Jessie's mom with her good hand and twisted away again.

"Yes, I do," said Evan. "The feed is in the barn, in the barrel to the left of the door. I fill the empty milk jug then shake it into the two feeders. And then I refill the pan with fresh water."

Grandma stopped struggling. "How do you know that?"

"I used to feed the chickens for you all the time," said Evan. Jessie thought his voice sounded funny, like it was being squeezed out of a toothpaste tube.

"Did you?" Her voice was quiet. She looked at Evan for a long time. "All right, then."

Evan walked out the back door and headed for the barn. Where was he going?

"Come on, Mom," said Mrs. Treski, helping Grandma out of her coat. Grandma was very quiet now. It looked as if she was concentrating really hard on a particularly difficult jigsaw puzzle.

Mrs. Treski led Grandma out of the kitchen. Jessie followed them into the living room and watched them go upstairs.

"You don't see that every day," Jessie murmured.

"You certainly don't," said Maxwell, right on cue, his eyes still glued to the TV set.

Seconds later Evan walked in through the front door.

"Why did you pretend to feed the chickens?" Jessie blurted out.

Evan pointed to the ceiling. "Is she upstairs?"

"Yeah, with Mom." Jessie looked at Evan's face. "There are no chickens, Evan!"

Evan shrugged. "Yeah, I know. I just thought it would be the easiest thing. I don't know."

"Is she pretending she doesn't know you again?"

"It's not pretending, Jessie!" Evan sounded angry. Why would he be angry? What had she done?

"That doesn't make sense," said Jessie. "You don't just forget someone in your family. That's not possible."

"Yeah, well, tell Grandma that. *You* can talk to her. She remembers *you.*" And now Jessie was positive that Evan was angry.

"None of this makes sense," said Jessie. "I'm going to go get Mom."

"No!" said Evan. "Leave her alone. She's taking care of Grandma."

"So?" said Jessie. "She can still talk to me." She headed for the stairs.

"Don't!" And the way he said it made Jessie stop and turn around. Maxwell laughed loudly at something that was on the TV, and Evan looked at him.

Then in a quiet voice, Evan said, "Why does he have to be here?"

"Because we're watching TV," Jessie said. What was wrong with Maxwell? Why didn't Evan want him around?

"Whatever," said Evan, and he headed for the kitchen. But before he left the room, he turned and said, "You were right. The bell's gone. We saw it, Grandma and me. Just before she went loopy."

Jessie went back to the couch and sat down next to Maxwell. Maybe there was something about the bell being gone that made Grandma forget. Jessie had been talking about the missing bell the first time Grandma went loopy. Now Grandma had *seen* that the bell was gone. Jessie wondered if the bell was part of the problem. If the bell were back where it belonged, the way it had always been, would Grandma be better?

"Tomorrow is New Year's Eve," Jessie said to Maxwell. "We've got to find that bell before midnight tomorrow."

Chapter 8

Out of Whack

The next morning, Pete showed Evan how to use a plumb bob to determine a true vertical. They were replacing the windows on the second floor, and they needed to get the window casings set in straight. It turned out to be a lot trickier than he thought.

"You can't just set 'em according to the studs," said Pete, "because this is an old house and the studs are cockeyed. And you can't use the floor or the ceiling to mark against, because the floor slopes and the ceiling sags. Old houses. Everything is out of whack."

Evan nodded. Old houses *and* old people, he thought.

Pete showed him how the plumb bob worked. It was a heavy metal weight tied to a length of string, and when you let the weight hang free, the string made a straight line "that goes all the way to the center of the earth," according to Pete.

"Really?" asked Evan.

"Yep. No matter where you go, no matter what you're standing on, if you have a plumb bob, it points straight to the center of the earth." He handed the plumb bob to Evan to try out. "That's gravity for you."

Evan hung the plumb bob from his finger like a yoyo. "That is so cool."

"Well, like my dad always said, 'Gravity is our friend.'"

Now that Pete had gone to the hardware store to buy a new box of galvanized screws, Evan was wandering around the house with the plumb bob to see if he could find even one thing that was the way it was supposed to be. It was surprising. Evan would look at a door and think it was straight, but then when he held up the string, he could see that it was crooked. The front door was out of whack. The railings on the stairs were out of whack. All the windows in the living room were out of whack.

"This house is crazy!" he announced loudly, even though there was no one there to hear him. His mother had gone into town to talk with the insurance agent handling the fire claim, Jessie was off with Maxwell, and Grandma was taking a nap.

"You can say that again!" A voice came from the kitchen. Evan walked in to find his grandmother wrapping her new scarf around her neck. Her injured arm was still in its sling, but she managed to get the scarf on with just one good hand.

"Grandma, you're supposed to be napping." He put the plumb bob on the kitchen counter next to the toaster and noticed that his mom's cell phone was plugged into the outlet, charging. His mother's phone was old, and the battery ran out just about every day. She kept saying she was going to replace it, but she never did.

"Says who?" said Grandma.

"Mom said."

"I'm not four, Evan. I know when I'm tired, and I know when I'm not."

Evan was so relieved to hear that she knew who he was, he smiled. But then he saw that she was putting on her snow boots, and the smile disappeared from his face. "Where are you going?"

"For a walk," said Grandma. "It makes me crazy being all cooped up."

"No," said Evan firmly. "Mom doesn't want you going out—" He was about to say *alone,* but he stopped himself.

"Since when does your mother tell me what to do?" Grandma had gotten both boots on her feet and was now reaching for her dark green barn jacket. She slipped her good arm through one sleeve and buttoned the loose coat over her injured arm. Evan was surprised to see how quickly and easily she managed the buttons. His grandmother really was amazing.

"Please don't go, Grandma," said Evan. "It's getting late. It'll be dark soon."

"I'll be quick. I just need to stretch my legs and see the sky. The trees are calling to me. Can't stand being in the house all day."

She was going. Evan could see that there was nothing he could do to stop her. That panicked feeling came back. Something bad was going to happen. How could he stop it? What was he supposed to do?

"I'll come with you," he said.

"Fine, but be quick. There's not much daylight left. I'll wait for you out front." Grandma pulled her hat on her head, looped Jessie's scarf once more around her neck, and walked out the back door.

Evan slipped his coat on first and checked to make sure he had both gloves in his pockets. Then he started to hunt for his boots. One of them was in the boot bin, but the second one was missing. He emptied out the entire bin, looked under the bench, and even checked in the kitchen, but the boot was nowhere to be seen. After five minutes had gone by, he finally thought to look between the clothes dryer and the wall, and there was his boot, wedged in tight. He wrestled it out and got it on his foot, then hurried out the back door and around the house to the front yard.

But Grandma was gone.

Chapter 9
Stakeout

"We need a map," said Jessie. She and Maxwell were at his house planning their stakeout. "Tonight's New Year's Eve, for crying out loud!" Luckily, it was early afternoon. There was still time, if they worked fast.

Maxwell had lots of drawing materials in his room: paper, markers, colored pencils, rulers, protractors. He even had one of those big slanting desks that architects use to draw up their plans. It was perfect. Jessie climbed up on the tall stool and began to draw.

There were only four houses within a mile of Grandma's house: the Uptons', Mrs. Lewis's, Maxwell's house, and the old Jansen house, which no

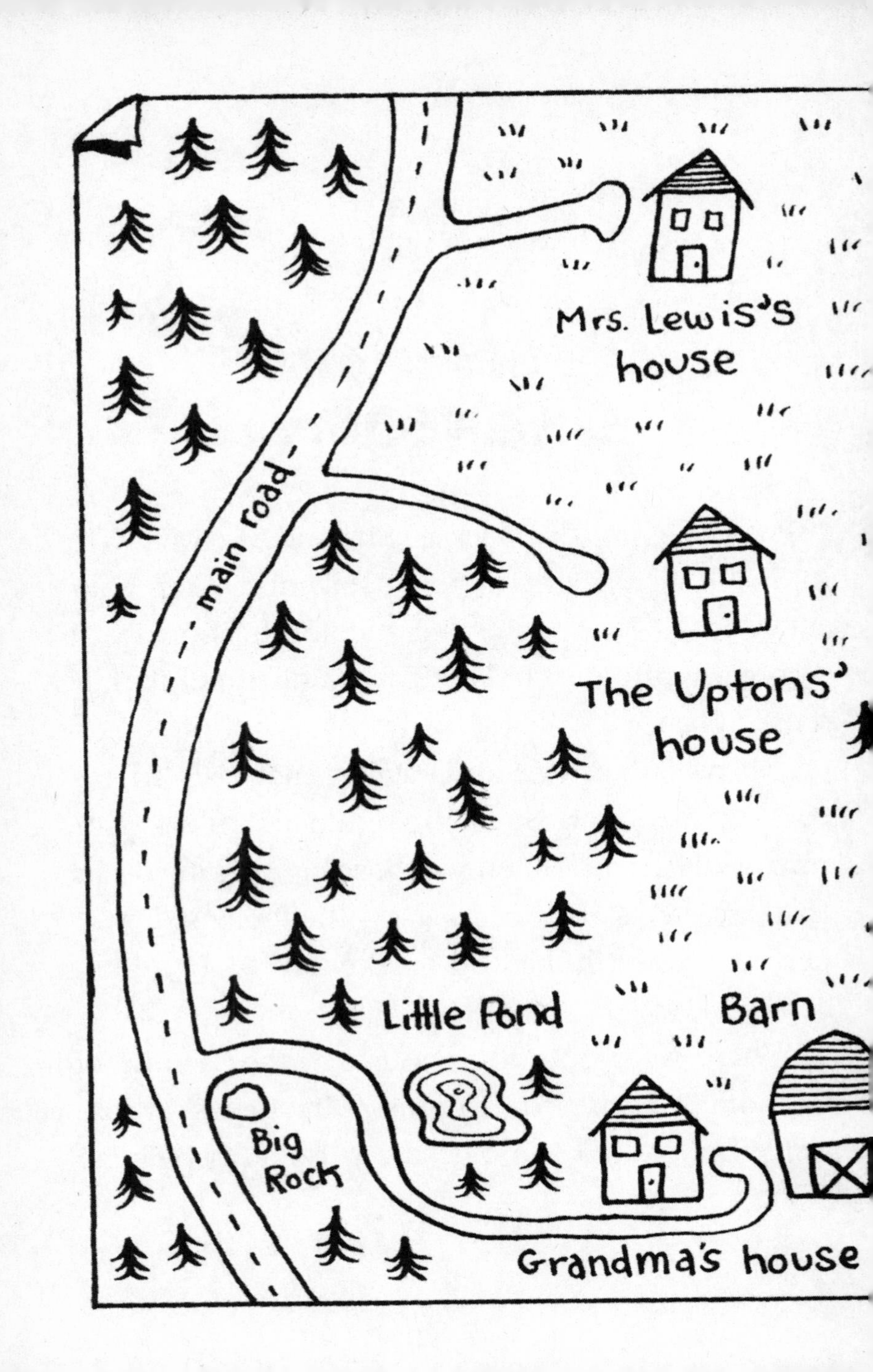

Mrs. Lewis's house
main road
The Uptons' house
Little Pond
Barn
Big Rock
Grandma's house

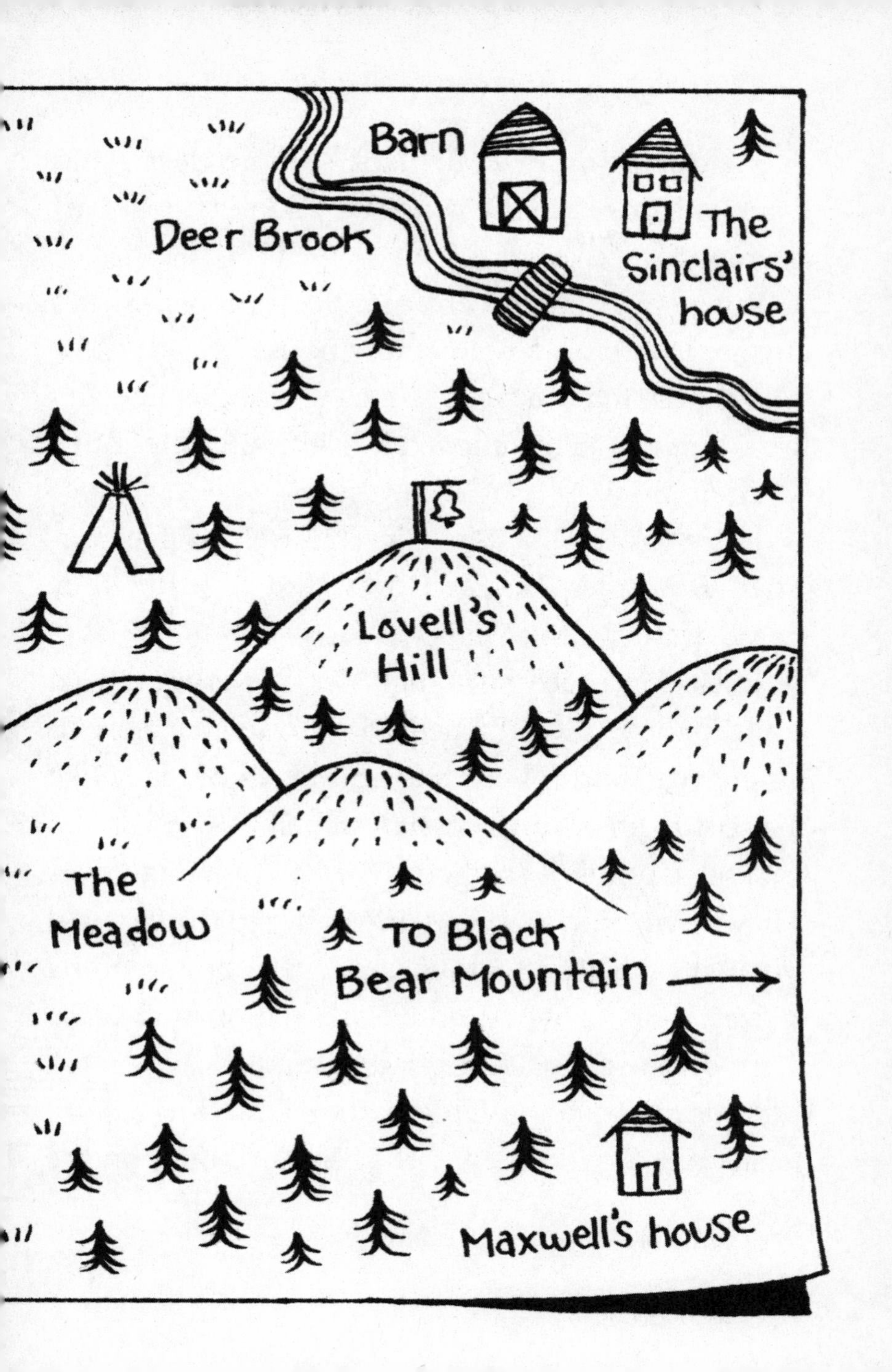
Barn
Deer Brook
The Sinclairs' house
Lovell's Hill
The Meadow
To Black Bear Mountain
Maxwell's house

one had lived in for years. Last summer Jessie and Evan had looked in the windows, and the house was as empty as a seashell.

But people moved around. So Jessie asked, "Is anyone living in that old empty house?"

Maxwell made a face. "That's where the Sinclairs live," he said. "They moved in right after me. But I was here first!"

Jessie wrote "The Sinclairs' House" on her map. Then she called Maxwell over, and together they stared at the piece of paper.

Jessie was pretty sure that Mrs. Lewis, who lived alone, hadn't taken the bell. Mrs. Lewis was close to ninety years old. There was no way an old lady like that could lift a hundred-pound bell.

The Uptons were good friends of Grandma's. They're the ones who had driven her to the hospital when she fell. The Uptons checked in on Grandma at least once a week, and Jessie's mom talked to them on the phone from time to time.

"I don't think the Uptons took Grandma's bell," Jessie said. She pointed to the Sinclair house on the other side of the bridge. "What are they like? Do they have any kids?"

"Mean boys," said Maxwell. He started rocking back and forth, taking that odd half-step with his right foot before shifting his weight back to his left. "Two of 'em. Mean, mean boys."

"What makes them mean?" asked Jessie, thinking back to the girls in her last-year class who had played a rotten joke on her. Jessie felt her face go hot, just remembering what they'd done.

Maxwell shook his head. "Won't say it. Mean boys. Both of 'em. Mean."

Jessie frowned. She needed Maxwell's help. If she was going to be Agent 99, she needed an Agent 86.

"Well, how old are they?"

"Jeff's in fifth grade and Mike's in fourth." Maxwell's rocking was getting faster, and then he stopped rocking and started walking in circles, snapping the fingers on his right hand like he was cracking a whip and making that strange puffing noise.

"Huh. They're not so big," said Jessie. But in her mind she imagined boys that towered over her, boys even taller than Evan, and he was one of the tallest boys in his fourth-grade class.

"They don't have to be big. They're mean," Maxwell said.

"You keep saying that," Jessie pointed out. "Stop repeating yourself. And sit down, for Pete's sake. You're making a lot of noise." Sometimes Maxwell could be very distracting.

Maxwell sat down on the edge of the bed, but he kept snapping his fingers and moving his feet back and forth, quietly blowing air through his lips.

"Did you ever hear them talk about Grandma's bell?" Jessie asked.

"Uh-huh. On the bus. They said they were going to take it."

"Really?" said Jessie. "They really *said* that? Why didn't you tell me?"

"You never asked."

"A person doesn't need to ask a question like that. A person should just know that that's the kind of information you'd tell a secret agent." Honestly, sometimes she just didn't get Maxwell. He was a smart kid, but there were times when he acted like he had rocks in his head.

"When did you hear them talking about Grandma's bell?"

"Wednesday. December eighth. At 2:23 p.m."

Jessie stared at him. "How do you remember that?"

Maxwell shrugged.

Jessie wasn't sure if Maxwell was going to turn out to be a terrible spy or the best spy who ever lived. Either way, they had their suspects, and that meant it was spying time.

Jessie pointed to the map. "That's where we need to go for the stakeout," she said. "We need to watch those boys. See what they do and where they hide their stuff."

"Nope, nope, nope," said Maxwell, shaking his head. "I'm not going there. They're mean boys."

"They'll never even see us. We'll hide in the woods," said Jessie. "We'll need bino-specs, though. Do you have anything like that?"

"I won't go," said Maxwell. "I won't go."

"Fine," said Jessie. "I'll go alone."

"Okay."

Jessie shook her head. "A friend is not supposed to make another friend go on a stakeout alone. You don't know anything about being a friend." Jessie thought of all the times Evan had explained to her the rules for getting along with other kids. Now, here she was explaining those rules to Maxwell. It felt weird.

But it didn't matter much, because Maxwell didn't seem to care one bit that she was calling him a bad friend. It seemed to Jessie that all he cared about was staying away from the Sinclair house. She thought for a minute and decided to try a different approach.

"I thought you said you were smart."

"I am," he said. "Maxwell Smart."

"Well, if you're really Maxwell Smart, then tell me what you always say to the Chief." Jessie started talking in a deep voice that she hoped sounded like the Chief on *Get Smart.* "Maxwell, you'll be facing every kind of danger imaginable . . ." Jessie waited for Maxwell to reply. She knew that Maxwell had memorized every line of dialogue in all 138 episodes of the show.

Maxwell whispered his line so quietly, Jessie couldn't hear it. "Louder!" she shouted. "Maxwell, you'll be facing every kind of danger imaginable . . ."

". . . and loving it!" shouted Maxwell. He broke into a big grin.

"You see! It'll be fun. We'll be just like Agent 99 and Maxwell Smart, and we'll find the bell!"

"We're not going to find the bell," said Maxwell.

"Don't be a pessimist," said Jessie, using one of her favorite big words. She headed for the door with the map in her hand. "We need to find binoculars. And flashlights. And maybe some kind of a weapon."

* * *

An hour later they were crouched behind a clump of young pine trees that grew on the edge of the woods. In front of them lay the bridge that crossed Deer Brook, and beyond that was the Sinclairs' house, their barn, and more woods.

Jessie stared through the binoculars they had borrowed from Maxwell's mom, but there wasn't much to see. She wished the binoculars were attached to a pair of eyeglasses, like the bino-specs on *Get Smart,* but there hadn't been time for that.

"We need to get closer," she said.

"Nuh-uh," said Maxwell, backing up slowly and bouncing a little.

Without waiting for Maxwell to agree, Jessie started running toward the house in a crouched-over position, keeping as low to the ground as she could. It was hard going because the snow was still deep, but she was determined to see what was happening inside the house.

When Jessie got to the porch steps, she scampered up and then pressed herself against the outside wall of the house. This, she thought, was the way a real agent would behave. She was good at this! It gave her a thrill to think that she was about to spy on a real suspect of a real crime.

She waited a minute without moving to see if Maxwell was going to follow her, but when she looked through her binoculars at the clump of pines she had just left, she could see that he was still there, hunkered down in the snow.

What a scaredy-cat! Of course, her own heart was pounding like a drum, but at least she had made it

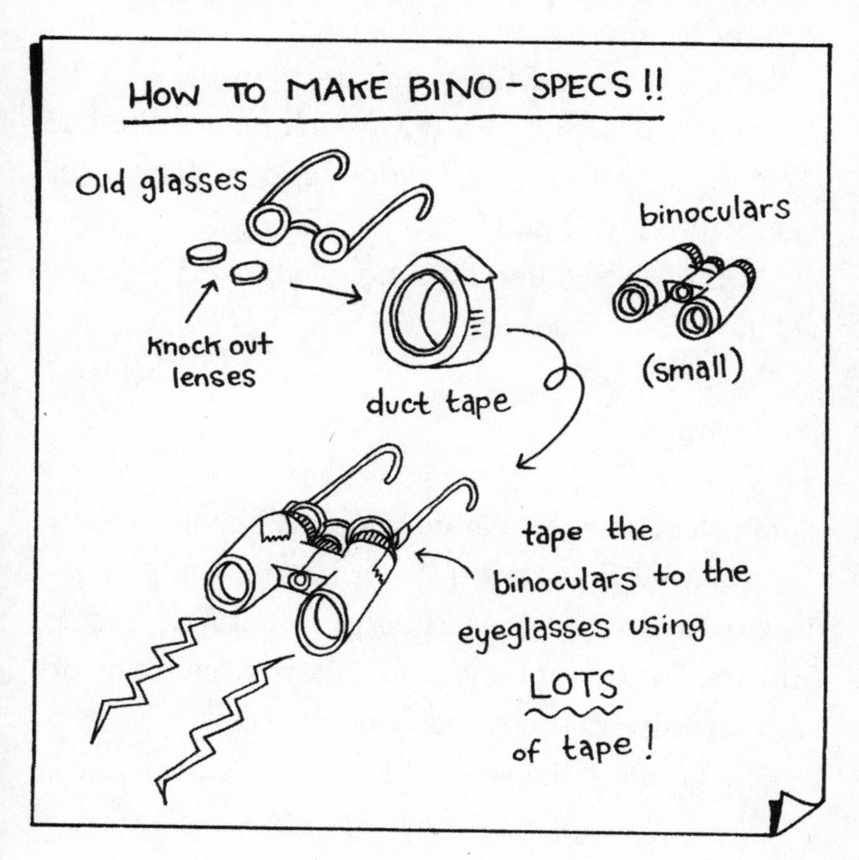

to the porch. What should she do now? Continue with the spy mission, or go back and get Maxwell? She thought about what the real Agent 99 would do, and she knew she didn't have a choice. Secret agents always stuck together. That was the whole point of having a partner.

Jessie tiptoed off the porch and ran back to the clump of pines. She found Maxwell just as she had left him, squatting in the snow and rocking back and forth on his heels.

"You have to come right now," she said.

"No!"

"Yes!"

"I won't."

"You will!"

He closed his eyes and shook his head furiously.

"Maxwell Smart, you listen to me. You've got a mission to do, and you're going to do it. We're spies. And they're the enemy. And this is what spies do. We creep up on the enemy, and we spy!"

She grabbed the sleeve of Maxwell's coat, and—

Jessie couldn't believe it—he came along. Just like that, he followed her across the yard and up the porch. In less than a minute, they were both pressed up against the wall with their heads just inches below the window.

But when they dared to lift their heads and peek in—there was nothing to see. They were just staring at a regular old dining room.

Silently, Jessie motioned with her hand for Maxwell to follow her. Crouched down, she crossed the porch to the window on the other side of the front door, and Maxwell came along right after her.

Again, they slowly raised their heads to look inside the window and saw . . . nothing. Just the living room, with no one in it.

Jessie sank down, pressing her back against the house. She looked at Maxwell, hoping he'd have a great idea, but he just looked like he wanted to go home. Spying was more difficult than Jessie had imagined.

Suddenly, there was a clattering and banging

noise inside the house. The front door flew open, and two boys in ski jackets and boots came charging out of the house and onto the porch.

Chapter 10
Shattering Glass

Evan started running down the driveway. Grandma would be easy to spot, he was sure. She was wearing a dark green coat that would stand out like a flag with all that white snow blanketing the ground. He wished he could follow her tracks, but Jessie and Maxwell and Pete and Evan had made so many footprints since yesterday, it was impossible to make sense out of the mishmash that covered the driveway.

And what if she hadn't stuck to the driveway? What if she was in the woods that spread out on both sides? Evan ran past Little Pond, looking left and right. The woods were shaded and filled with the shifting shadows of brown and green cast by tall pine trees. The sun was low in the sky, and the woods seemed to be sprouting strange shapes right before his eyes. If Grandma had stopped to sit down, if she was hurt and lying on the ground surrounded by the thickness and silence of those trees, he would never see her.

He started to run faster. He thought of calling out, but a voice inside told him not to. Maybe Grandma had forgotten who he was again. Maybe she would be afraid of him. If she heard his voice calling, she might hide, and then he would never find her.

The thought banged against the inside of his skull with every crashing step he took. It was cold, and it was getting dark. She was old and didn't remember things right. People died up here in the mountains. Kids lost in a snowstorm. Grownups when their cars broke down. Hikers who left the trails and became disoriented. Evan had heard the stories. People died up here.

Evan kept running. The driveway was long and curved and stretched for over half a mile before reaching the road. He was breathing hard, and each breath felt like a rusty knife sawing through his lungs. His eyes stung from the cold, and two puddles of snot collected under his nostrils. But he kept running. Running toward the road. How far could she have gotten? As far as the road? She was wearing a dark green coat. No one would be able to see that coat if she was walking on the side of the road after dark. What if a car came around a curve too fast?

When Evan reached the Big Rock, he heard a car—the crunch and grind of its wheels as it turned from the main road onto the driveway. Mom! Evan would have screamed if his throat weren't so dry and raw from running in the cold. He waved his arms wildly, running toward the road.

But it wasn't his mother's car. It was Pete's truck, and Pete rolled down his window to find out why Evan was acting like a crazy person in the middle of the road. Breathing hard, trying to keep from crying, Evan explained.

Pete listened seriously. "Okay, first thing, let's call your mom."

"She doesn't have her cell phone with her—she

left it at home! And I don't know exactly where she is. Somewhere in town. Meeting with an insurance agent."

Pete nodded his head slowly, letting this information sink in.

"All right, then. Here's the plan. Someone needs to stay at the house. Can you do that? Can you be the person who answers the phone if anyone calls and who waits there in case your grandmother comes back on her own?"

Evan nodded his head.

"I'll call the police, and they'll put together a search. When's your mom expected back?"

Evan shook his head. "She said by dinnertime."

"I think I better drive into town and track her down," said Pete. "If she gets back before I do, have her call me on my cell, okay?"

"Okay." Evan was glad Pete was here, giving orders. Still, nothing Pete had said so far made Evan feel like Grandma was any closer to being found.

"I'll take you back to the house," said Pete.

"No, I'll walk," said Evan. He wanted Pete to go get his mother as soon as possible. And there was nothing waiting back at the house for him. Evan was sure of that.

Pete backed up the truck to the road and then spun the wheel and roared off. Evan started walking slowly toward the house. With every step he took, he became more convinced that Grandma was out in the woods, out in the falling darkness, out in the cold. And he couldn't help feeling that it was his fault. He should have convinced her not to go for a walk. He should have talked her into waiting with him in the mudroom. He should have found his boot more quickly. Heard her leaving. Figured out which way she'd gone. Not been the one she forgot. The one she didn't like.

When Evan got back to the house, he went first to the barn. No one was there. Then he stood in the front yard, the last place Grandma had been, and stared at the house. No lights were on. Grandma wasn't back. Pete had told him to wait inside. That was his job. And over the last few days, Pete had taught him the importance of each man doing his job and doing it well.

But what if Grandma had gone to the bell? What

if the bell had "called to her"? That's what Grandma said. Sometimes things called to her, and she had to follow their voices. A bird. A cluster of irises. The pond. The moon. All these things called to Grandma from time to time. And she always went when she was called.

Evan dove into the woods, finding the path that led through the trees to Lovell's Hill. The sun was dipping below Black Bear Mountain and everything had gone flat and gray, but Evan knew the path. He hurried until he made it to the top of the steep rise where the old oak crossbeam stood.

Evan looked around. Black Bear Mountain rose behind him like a giant tidal wave. The trees looked like soldiers guarding a gate. The snow under his feet seemed to deaden all sound, and the cold was beginning to creep up into his boots and snake its way up his legs.

Evan stared at the crossbeam, empty like an eye socket. Grandma wasn't here. The bell wasn't here. Nothing was the way it was supposed to be. Nothing was ever going to be the way it was supposed to be.

Evan had that feeling that he got sometimes—that out-of-nowhere feeling—of missing his dad. His dad was supposed to be here in an emergency. But his dad wasn't here and hadn't been for a long time. Sometimes he sent e-mails with pictures attached of all the places he traveled for work, and sometimes he sent gifts—a felt hat from Pakistan or a tiny bottle made out of blue glass from Afghanistan. But Evan hadn't seen his dad in almost a year.

And suddenly Evan knew who it was he needed to help him find Grandma. It wasn't his father. It wasn't his mother. He needed someone who would treat it like a math problem, who would keep a clear head. Someone who would be able to solve the puzzle. He needed Jessie.

Evan knew the way to Maxwell's house and figured he could be there in ten minutes if he ran the whole way. But as he turned to head down the hill, the air splintered with sound—first a scream and then the noise of shattering glass. The sound came from the direction of the little bridge that crossed Deer Brook. Evan started to run.

Chapter 11

Agent 99 Goes Solo

Jessie felt as if someone had waved a wand and turned her entire body to stone. Every muscle froze; the air locked in her lungs; even her eyes refused to blink. She pressed her back against the wall of the house and prayed to become invisible.

The two boys, though, never turned around. They raced off the porch without a single backward glance and ran toward the barn. Within ten seconds they were gone, and Jessie and Maxwell were left alone on the wide wooden porch.

"That was a close one," whispered Jessie, surprised her voice was working at all.

But Maxwell didn't say anything. His face had gone sort of grayish white, and his eyes kept staring where the boys had been.

Finally he whispered, "They would have killed us if they found us."

"They would not!" Jessie whispered back. "Maybe they would have yelled and told their mother, and maybe we would have gotten in trouble, but they would not have killed us."

"You don't know them!" said Maxwell, his voice rising dangerously.

"Shhh! You want to get us caught? Jeepers, Maxwell, act like a spy, would you?"

Maxwell stood up and started walking in circles. Jessie stared through her binoculars at the barn.

"They were carrying stuff," she said. "Did you notice?" Jessie had seen that both boys had something in their hands, but she'd been too scared to see what.

"A shoebox and a hammer," said Maxwell, still walking. "Jeff had the shoebox. Mike had the hammer."

"Wow. You *are* a good spy," said Jessie. She wished

she'd noticed those things, but it had all happened so fast.

Jessie looked at the barn again. Maxwell started to walk slower and slower, and then he stopped and just stood in one spot, rocking back and forth.

"We need to go see what they're doing in that barn," said Jessie.

Maxwell started shaking his head.

"Yes, we do," she said. "I bet that's where they hide things. I bet they've got a secret compartment in that barn, and that's where they are right now, and if we find that secret compartment, we'll find the bell."

"No," said Maxwell. "No, we won't. We will not find the bell in that barn."

"Well, we're going to find something, that's for sure," said Jessie. "Come on." She scooted off the porch in her low-to-the-ground crouch and hurried across the open front yard to the barn. One quick glance over her shoulder told her that Maxwell was staying behind. She'd have to do this bit of spying alone. *Agent 99 goes solo.*

The large sliding door to the barn was open just

a foot, but Jessie didn't want to spy from there. If the boys came barreling out the door, she'd get caught for sure, and she could still remember what it felt like to be on the porch, pressed up against the wall of the house, with nowhere to hide. She could hear music coming from inside the barn, a pop song that she recognized.

Nope, this time she was going to be smart. She and Evan had circled this barn a dozen times over the years. She knew there were windows on the sides and back of the barn. She walked to the left until she came to the first of two small windows. The boys had turned on all the overhead lights—rows and rows of them, which lit up the barn like a stage. This was lucky for her, because it made it much easier to see inside the barn, and she knew that with the fading daylight she would be almost invisible if the boys looked up.

She peeked her head around to look in the barn, but all she could see was the usual stuff: a tractor, old tools hanging on the wall, a workbench with piles of magazines all over it, baled hay. It looked like her grandma's barn. Jessie couldn't see the boys anywhere. But she could hear hammering.

She crouched down again and scuttled over to the second window, but she still couldn't see the boys. The hammering stopped, and then it started up again.

Jessie continued to walk around the outside of the barn. She was starting to think she might need to sneak inside the barn itself, when she popped her head up at the single small window on the back of the barn and came practically face-to-face with the older of the two boys. It was as if she was standing just three feet away from him and he was looking right at her.

Jessie was so surprised, she immediately ducked her head back down and waited to hear a shout from the boy. But the hammering continued, and Jessie realized that the bright light inside and the growing darkness outside had turned the window into a one-way mirror. She could peek in without being seen.

Slowly, she inched her head up.

Jeff and Mike were in one of the stalls that ran along the back of the barn. The ceiling here was low, the floor covered in rough wood. Jessie looked around and realized the compartment was used for storing firewood. The split firewood was stacked in racks that jutted out of one of the side walls of the small room. The racks were made of long two-by-fours nailed into the floor and the ceiling. The room looked dirty and creepy to Jessie, but it was a perfect place to hide something.

Both boys were standing in front of the middle rack. Jessie could see that they had pounded a couple of nails into the two-by-fours along with some thin splints of wood that formed an *X*. Two strings dangled from the nails. The boys were pounding something else onto the two-by-fours, but Jessie couldn't see what it was. The younger one—Mike—held the nail steady, while the older one—Jeff—hammered it in. She reached into her backpack and took out her notebook to make a quick diagram. This might be important information she was gathering, and she wanted to get it right.

As she watched, Jessie figured out what the boys were nailing to the board: two large spools of thread, each one set on a nail so that it could turn easily. She added the spools to her diagram.

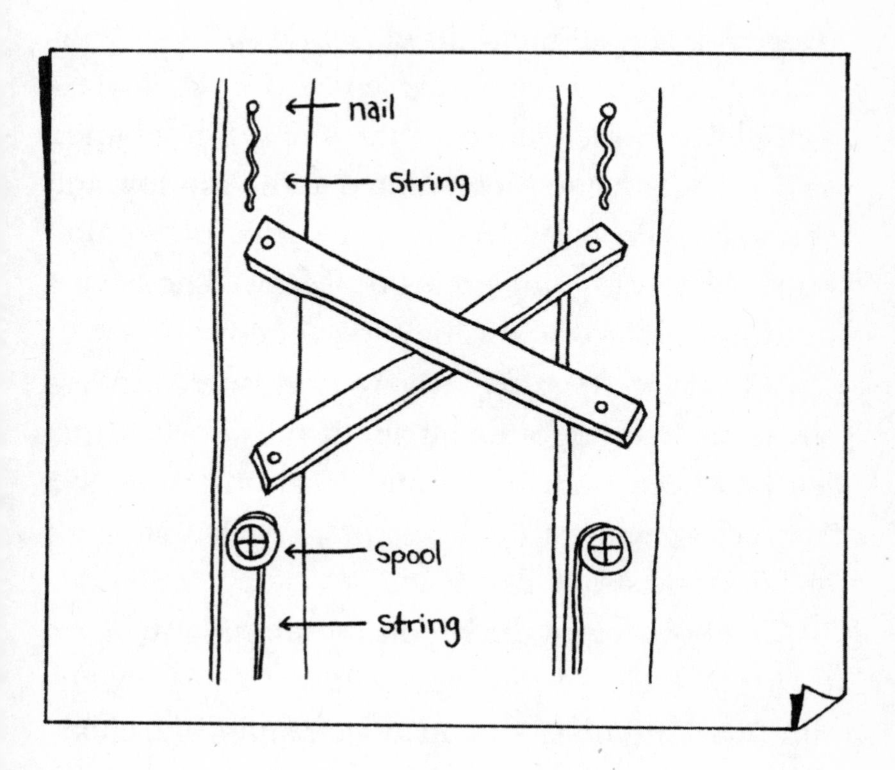

"What are they doing?" a voice whispered nearby.

Jessie nearly dropped her pencil, she was so startled. In the dim light, she could just see Maxwell peeking around the corner of the barn. He'd snuck up close to her without her even hearing him! He really did have all the skills of a good spy.

She motioned for him to come over, and Maxwell glided noiselessly over the snow. She pointed to her diagram and then pointed at the window and shrugged her shoulders to show that she didn't know what was going on inside. Maxwell poked his head up and looked through the window.

"What's in the box?" Maxwell whispered to Jessie. Jessie had forgotten all about the shoebox that Jeff had been carrying before. It sat on the floor a few feet away from the boys with a rock resting on its lid. Jessie shook her head.

The boys tested the spools by spinning them on their nails. The spools spun wildly, making a whirring, clacking noise that made Jeff and Mike laugh. Jessie was intrigued. The boys didn't seem mean at all! They were building something new, and Jessie liked to do that, too—whether it was making a complicated track for racing marbles or a lemonade stand with hand-painted signs and a canopy.

Next to her, Maxwell started to make his puffing sound. Jessie looked over at him and shook her head sharply. If they blew this stakeout, they weren't going to get a second chance to find the bell before tonight. Maxwell put a hand over his own mouth and started to rock back and forth. His eyes were glued to the window like he was watching a horror movie.

Jessie turned back in time to see Mike pick up the shoebox and reach a hand under the lid. Jeff crowded close to Mike, and for a minute, Jessie couldn't see what they were doing.

Then Mike held up his hands, and Jessie could see that he was holding a frog—a live frog! Its back legs kicked a couple of times, dangling below Mike's hands. Mike held the frog up while Jeff tied one of the strings attached to the nail to one of the frog's front legs. Then he tied the other string to the other front leg. Jessie couldn't figure out what they were planning to do. Maxwell started to make a noise Jessie had never heard from him. It was like a moan, but it came out in short bursts. The hand over his mouth muffled the sound, but Jessie was still worried the boys would hear it. There was nothing she could do, though. She couldn't take her eyes off the scene inside the barn.

Now the frog was dangling by its front legs, its back pressed against the wooden splints the boys had hammered into place, its pale green belly facing out. It tried to kick itself free, but its powerful hind legs had nothing to push against.

The boys set to work on the frog's jumping legs. Jeff grabbed the left leg and started to wrap the thread from one of the spools around it. Mike did the same with the right leg and the other spool. Jessie started to see a picture in her head, a picture of how the spools would turn, how the strings would get tighter, how the legs of the frog would stretch and stretch and stretch until . . .

Out of the corner of her eye, Jessie saw Maxwell press his other hand over his mouth. The sounds from his mouth were coming out faster and louder. Jessie felt like she was deep underwater—everywhere heaviness pressed on her. Her legs felt heavy. Her arms felt heavy. Her mouth felt sealed shut, as if a big hand had clamped down on it. She couldn't move. She couldn't think.

Jeff began to turn the spool on the left as Mike turned the one on the right. The frog began to kick furiously, but soon the kicks became little quivers as the strings pulled in all directions. And then the quivering stopped. The frog couldn't move. All four legs were stretched as far as they could go. Only the soft green belly of the frog moved, vibrating in and out, as if its heart would beat right out of its chest. And the frog's mouth opened and closed, in what looked to Jessie like a silent scream.

Suddenly, there *was* a scream, and Jessie had the strange thought that it came from the frog! It was a cry like Jessie had never heard before. She turned and saw Maxwell screaming wildly as he kicked at the snow, looking for something buried underneath. When he found what he wanted—a rock the size of his fist—he picked it up and hurled it through the window. The glass smashed to pieces, and Jessie jumped back. Maxwell continued to scream as if he were being skinned alive.

And then he bolted, running back over the bridge, leaving Jessie in the dark with the two Sinclair boys staring right at her through the hole in the shattered glass.

Chapter 12
A Fair Fight

Evan ran toward the bridge, stumbling in the deepening darkness. On the other side, he could see someone running toward him, but the light was so dim, he couldn't tell who it was. The person was running as if a wild animal were chasing it, arms clawing madly at the air, legs galloping down the hill toward the bridge. Evan had to stop abruptly at the bridge to prevent a collision.

That's when he saw it was Maxwell. But Maxwell was supposed to be with Jessie. Where was Jessie? Who had screamed? What broke the glass?

"Maxwell, what happened?" Evan shouted, but Maxwell wasn't stopping. He barreled over the bridge, running past Evan as if Evan didn't even exist.

"Stop! Stop!" Evan yelled, but it seemed like Maxwell never heard him. He ran up the hill and into the woods, and then he was out of sight.

Evan turned and raced over the bridge and up the hill where Maxwell had come from. There was a house up here, the old Jansen house. He saw that the lights were on, so he headed for the porch but then stopped. He heard voices. Coming from behind the barn. And one of them was Jessie's.

When Evan rounded the back corner of the barn, he practically ran over his little sister. She was standing with her legs apart, buried halfway up to her knees in the deep snow, with both arms crooked at the elbow. In each hand, she held a rock the size of a baseball.

In front of her were two boys. It took Evan just a split second to size them up. The bigger one looked to be just about Evan's size; the other one wasn't much smaller. When Jessie saw Evan, she took three quick steps backwards but kept the rocks held tightly in her fists. She'd been holding her own against the boys—that was Jessie!—but Evan could tell she was scared.

"Hey!" Evan shouted, and took a step toward the boys.

"Is this your brother?" shouted the older boy at Jessie. "He's not so big! We could beat him up with our hands tied behind our backs." The younger boy laughed and said, "Yeah!"

"Come on, then," said Evan. He made a move toward the older boy, pushing his chest out and balling up his fists, but just then a rock landed on the ground right between them.

"Stop it!" said Jessie. "Fighting is for morons!"

"Yeah, like that moron who broke our window!"

"He's not a moron. You're the morons! It's disgusting what you were doing!"

"What is going on?" shouted Evan.

"They were torturing a frog in there, Evan!" Jessie said, and Evan could tell she was on the very edge of crying. "Maxwell and me were spying on them—"

"Yeah, you were spying on us. On our property—"

"So what! You should go to jail for what you did!"

"You're the one who's going to jail! Trespassing. Spying. Breaking windows!"

"Shut up!" Evan yelled, and everyone did. "Jessie, did you break the window?"

"No. Maxwell broke the window. Because they had a frog tied up and were trying to pull its legs off. While it was still *alive.*"

Evan looked at the two boys, and suddenly they didn't seem to have anything to say. The older one looked at the ground. The younger one looked at the older one, and then he looked down at the ground, too.

Evan shook his head. "That is *sick.* That is really, really sick." Evan was a tough kid who liked guts and gore as much as anyone. But the thought of hurting a real animal made his stomach turn.

"It's our property. We can do whatever we want on it. And you're still trespassing." The older boy made a move toward Evan, and the younger one backed him up from behind.

Evan stepped forward to show he wasn't afraid. But two of them at once. That was going to be hard, and Evan didn't have a lot of experience with fighting. He tightened his fists at his sides, wishing he had one of his friends from home. Paul or Jack or even Scott Spencer. It would be a fair fight if it were two against two.

Wham. Another rock came sailing at them, and this time it hit the older boy in the shoulder.

"Jeez, what are you doing?" he shouted. "You can't throw rocks."

"Who says?" said Jessie. "Show me the rule book." Her voice sounded funny, and Evan could tell she was shaking. But there she was, standing up to those boys. Just like she'd stood up to Scott Spencer when she put him on trial for stealing the lemonade money. She might be the smallest fourth-grader in the world because she'd skipped a grade, but Jessie had bossed around the whole class. When it came to justice, she was fearless. Maybe this was going to be a fair fight after all.

"Hold her down," said the older boy to the younger boy, and as soon as the smaller one took a step toward Jessie, Evan let loose. He shoved the younger boy so hard, the kid fell to the ground, then he turned on the older boy with both his hands up, ready to swing. The older boy quickly backed away.

"Hey, calm down. It's no big deal," he said. "Jeez, you two are really a pain in the neck. Just take your stupid sister and get out of here."

Evan kept his fists up in front of him, standing his ground. Out of the corner of his eye, he could see that the younger brother was crying but had gotten up on his feet. Bullies! It was like his mother said—stand up to them and they always back down.

"Come on, Jess," said Evan, lowering his hands halfway.

"No," said Jessie.

Evan could see that she was holding two more rocks, one in each hand. *No? What was she thinking?*

"Jess, we're going."

"Not until we get that frog out of there."

The older boy took a step forward. "You are *not* going inside our barn. There is no way I'm letting you in there."

Evan could tell the boy meant it. You didn't mess

with farm families and their property. Evan had spent enough time in these woods to know that. Jessie was pushing their luck, and she was going to get them both in a lot of trouble.

But Jessie didn't care. "I'm going to break every window in your barn until your mother comes out here to see what all the noise is, and then *you* can tell her what you're doing in there."

Oh man, thought Evan, feeling his insides crumple up. *Now we're going to get murdered.*

"If you throw even one more rock—" The boy took a step toward Jessie. Evan took a step toward the boy. The younger kid circled around behind Evan. *Here it comes,* thought Evan.

But a voice called out. "Jeff! Mike! Where are you?" It was a woman's voice, and it came from the direction of the house.

"Good!" said Jessie. "Now you have to go inside, or she's going to come looking for you. And then what? Huh?"

To Evan's surprise, the older boy hesitated. The younger boy stopped, too—frozen.

"Right now, you two!" The voice rolled across the yard like a bowling ball. "If I have to call you a second time, you'll be sorry I did!"

The younger boy took off.

The older boy looked at Evan and Jessie and said, "You better be gone in five minutes. I'm going to come back out here, and you better be gone." He started walking toward the house, but once he passed the barn, Evan saw that he broke into a run and didn't stop until he was on the porch. He disappeared inside the house, swallowed up by the front door.

Before Evan could say anything, Jessie started to run inside the barn. "We have to get that frog out of there!"

But when they got inside the barn and found their way to the wood storage room, the frog looked more dead than alive. It was hanging by its front legs, its back legs making weak kicking movements that seemed like the feeble waving of a surrender flag. Jessie didn't want to touch the frog, so Evan held the frog's body in his hands while Jessie plucked at the strings tied to each leg. When they got the last one off, Evan put the frog down on the dirt floor of the barn.

It was as if the frog had forgotten how to move. It wiggled its back legs, but couldn't seem to get a solid footing on the cold ground. First one leg and then the other shot out from its body, kicking at the air, but unable to move forward. Evan and Jessie watched, waiting.

"It's going to die," said Jessie, and Evan thought she was probably right. The frog had forgotten how to jump, or maybe its legs had been broken or permanently damaged in some way. Evan felt a sudden wave of sadness for all the things in the world that were damaged and broken.

Evan looked down at the frog and said, "We can't just leave it here to die. We need to take it home." But what he was thinking was, *And put it out of its misery.* He reached down to pick up the small animal, and when his hand was just an inch away, the frog leaped through the air and disappeared under the woodpile.

"Hey!" said Jessie. "He's okay! Did you see him jump? Wow!"

Jessie smiled at Evan, and he wanted to smile back, but he couldn't. The dark thought was still banging inside his head. "C'mon," he said. "We gotta go. And we don't have a lot of time."

Chapter 13
The Missing Bell

They went back to the top of Lovell's Hill, where the empty crossbeam stood, because they needed a place to start their search and Jessie couldn't think of anywhere else. Night had fallen, and a thick cover of clouds hung low in the sky. Luckily, Jessie had brought a flashlight on the stakeout. The thin yellow beam illuminated the ground just enough for them to make their way.

At the top of the hill, Jessie flashed the light ahead of her. There was the heavy wooden crossbeam with its empty space where the bell should have hung.

The missing bell. What a lousy spy she'd turned out to be! She hadn't learned a thing on the stakeout. She still didn't have any proof that the Sinclair boys had stolen the bell in the first place. And Maxwell had ended up half out of his mind, running off—to where? Where was Maxwell now? Was he missing, too?

"Maybe Grandma was here," said Jessie, skipping the flashlight beam over the ground. There were hundreds of footprints in the snow. Both Jessie and Maxwell had crossed this hill several times over the last few days, and Evan had come straight over the hill when he heard Maxwell's scream and the broken glass. There were footprints everywhere. The ground was a tangled-up dance of feet.

"Think, Jessie," said Evan. "It's like a puzzle. You're good at puzzles. Where would she go?"

Jessie looked up toward Black Bear Mountain, but there was no way she could see it in the darkness. The woods behind her were a thick brushstroke of blackness, too. Blackness in front of her. Blackness behind her. Where could Grandma be in all that dark?

Something cold and wet landed on Jessie's cheek. Then another and another. It was beginning to snow.

"Oh, Grandma," said Jessie, quietly.

"C'mon, Jess," said Evan. "You can think this out. I know you can."

In her mind, Jessie made a list. "She wouldn't walk on the road. She hates walking on the road. So forget that. She didn't go to a neighbor, because they would have brought her back. She's not in the barn?"

"I checked."

"Don't you think she's on the farm somewhere?"

Evan nodded his head. "Yeah, but where?" It was a big farm. A hundred acres.

"Let's go back to where she started. The house. And then we'll take the backward loop." That was Grandma's favorite walk, the one that took you all the way to the foot of Black Bear Mountain and then looped back through the woods, up the hill to the New Year's Eve bell. Jessie had done that walk a hundred times with Grandma.

When they got to the dark house, Evan ran inside to grab an extra flashlight and leave a note for their mother. Then they both strapped on snowshoes—the snow was coming down faster now—and headed down the path.

MOM
Jessie and I are looking
for grandma. Don't worry.
We'll stay close to The
house. We have Snowshoes
and we'll Stick together Evan

It was hard going. Evan led the way, and Jessie trudged behind. As they walked, they swung the beams of their flashlights from the path, to the woods on the left, back to the path, and then over to the woods on the right. Jessie called out "Grandma!" from time to time. Once she heard something scrabbling close to her feet, but she told herself it was just a squirrel or maybe a rabbit. Nothing to be afraid of. Still, she picked up her pace so that she was right behind Evan—so close that the tip of her snowshoe caught the tail of his and caused him to stumble. She thought he was going to turn around and yell at her, but he didn't. He just kept going.

When they reached the foot of Black Bear Mountain, Jessie was hot and sweaty under her ski hat, her bangs plastered to her forehead. Her mittened fingers were damp, too, but her cheeks were stinging from the cold.

Jessie wiped her hand across her face. "We haven't found her yet," she said, pausing to rest at the bend in the path that turned away from the mountain and into the woods. She wanted Evan to say something back, something that would give them hope. But Evan didn't say anything. He just shone his light in a circle all around them. The feeble yellow beam danced across trees and rocks and drifts of snow—snow everywhere, covering everything and falling thicker and faster now.

They kept on walking. Now they were cutting

through the woods that covered the far side of Lovell's Hill. There wasn't even a real path here. The only way to navigate was to look for the marked trees, but the markings were invisible in the pitch-black. Even when they focused the beams of their flashlights directly on the trunks of the trees, the falling snow made it impossible to see.

"Grandma!" Jessie called out, but more softly now. The woods were so silent that every sound seemed amplified. Evan kept stopping. Jessie could tell he was trying to get his bearings. It was easy to veer off course in the woods, even in the daytime. At night, with no moon to guide by, it would take all their concentration to find their way to the top of the hill.

Where are you, Grandma?

When they reached the top of the hill, they stood on either side of the heavy wooden crossbeam and stared at the darkness all around them.

"Evan?" said Jessie. "I don't know where she is." Jessie felt a heaviness sink into her body, and she knew she was not going to be able to solve this puzzle. She had failed.

Evan's voice came out weak and bedraggled. "You'll figure it out, Jessie. I know you will."

Jessie looked at her big brother and saw that he was crying. There were wet patches on his cheeks, and his long eyelashes glistened in the dim glow of the flashlight.

"Why are you crying?" asked Jessie.

"Because I'm cold! And I'm scared! And—." Evan waved his arms at the nothingness all around them."It's dark. It's dark, Jessie. And she's all alone out there somewhere. And I bet she's feeling like I am. Cold and scared and afraid of the dark."

Jessie thought about this. This was new information, and she tried to add it to the puzzle.

"Well, if she's cold . . . then she's going to want to go someplace warm," said Jessie. "And if she's scared, then I guess . . ." Jessie thought about the places she went when she was feeling frightened or overwhelmed: the nurse's office at school, her bedroom, the pages of a favorite book. "She probably wants to hide away somewhere."

What kind of place was like that on the farm? A place that was warm. A place that was hidden away.

A place that made you feel safe. Jessie tried to imagine such a place. She closed her eyes so she could concentrate. She tricked her brain into feeling cozy and safe and protected.

Then she opened her eyes and looked at Evan. "I know where she is."

Chapter 14
Waiting for a Bus

They couldn't find the tepee. If you'd asked Evan yesterday, he would have said, *I can find that tepee blindfolded.* But here they were, as good as blind-folded because of the darkness, and Evan had no idea where to look. He and Jessie wandered through the woods, flashing their lights in every direction, but either they'd gone too far or not far enough, because the tepee wasn't there.

What if they couldn't find it in the dark? Evan knew his grandmother wouldn't survive a night out in the cold like this. Even if the police managed to get together a search party soon—and Evan hadn't seen a single flashlight or heard any voices in the woods yet—it might be too late by the time they found her. His grandmother was old, and she had a broken wrist. She got confused. She needed help. He started walking faster, but he had no idea if he was getting closer to the tepee or farther away.

"Stop," said Jessie. "We need a system. We can't just keep walking around hoping we're going to find it."

So they followed their tracks back to the bell and stared at the edge of the woods they had just come out of.

"Where's the Lightning Tree?" asked Evan. They swept their flashlight beams back and forth, but they couldn't see through the thick falling snow. So they split up, each starting at one edge of the woods and working their way to the middle, checking each tree that they came to.

Finally, Evan said, "I found it!" And he had. Up close, the tree was unmistakable, burned black and naked without any branches except the single stubby one. The branch pointed their way into the woods, and they plunged deeper and deeper in. Evan kept telling himself, *We're getting closer, we're getting closer,* but it seemed to him that they were taking way too long to find Grandma.

"There it is," said Jessie, pointing with her flashlight through the trees.

And there it was. Just where it had always been. The tepee they'd built the summer before last. The tepee that was strong enough to survive a hundred winters. Evan broke into an awkward run, his snowshoes flopping and slapping the ground. When he reached the opening, he stopped, suddenly afraid to see what was inside.

Jessie caught up behind him, looked at him, then reached out to pull back the tarp.

"No!" said Evan, grabbing her hand and pulling it back. He didn't know what they would find inside, but if it was bad, he didn't want Jessie seeing it first.

He took a step forward so that his body blocked Jessie's view, then he slowly pulled back the top edge of the tarp, just enough for him to poke his flashlight inside and peer into the circle of light.

There was Grandma.

Sitting on the ground, cross-legged.

Her eyes blinked like an owl's, caught in an unexpected light. How long had she been sitting like that?

"Hi," said Evan, afraid to call her *Grandma* in case that spooked her. It felt to him as though she were standing on the edge of a cliff and any sudden movement could topple her over. He noticed that her hat was crooked and Jessie's scarf dangled from one shoulder.

"Is the bus here?" asked Grandma. "I've been waiting for hours."

"Grandma!" shouted Jessie from behind Evan. Suddenly he felt Jessie shoving his body out of the way, sliding past him and into the tepee. He wanted to grab her and keep her back, but he was holding the flashlight and the tarp, and she slipped by before he could stop her.

"Why are you here, Grandma?" Jessie was practically shouting, or at least it seemed that way to Evan. "Why didn't you come home?"

Grandma looked bewildered. "I'm waiting for the bus. It's been hours. What's the delay?"

"What are you talking about Grandma? There's no bus!"

"No bus! What do you mean? Of course, there's a bus. I take this bus three times a week."

"Grandma," said Jessie, sounding like she was about to cry. "Stop it. Stop pretending. It isn't funny!"

Grandma gave Jessie a disapproving stare. "Who are you? Why are you yelling at me? Where's the bus?"

"Evan!" yelled Jessie, and now she was crying. Evan could see the first few tears pooling up in her eyes, and he knew if she really got going, there would be no stopping her. She hardly ever cried, but when she did, it was a thunderstorm.

"Jess, it's okay," said Evan, pulling on her arm. She tried to shake her arm free, but he got a good firm hold of her. "C'mon. Come out here."

She let him pull her out of the tepee, where they stood side by side in the falling snow. "She's tired," he said. "And she's old. This is how it is now. We have to get used to it."

"No! No, no, no!" said Jessie, shaking her head.

"I won't get used to it. I'll never get used to it! She doesn't even know me!"

"Yeah, she does," said Evan. "Somewhere in her brain she knows exactly who you are. She just can't reach it right now. It's like my bedroom at Grandma's house. It's still there. We just can't get to it for a while. It's off-limits. But she'll remember you again. When she's not so cold and tired."

"I hate this," whispered Jessie.

He bent his head closer to hers. "I know. But look, we've got to get her home. Can you go in there and talk to her? Get her to come out?"

Jessie shook her head. "I can't. I can't."

"Okay," said Evan. "It's okay. You don't have to. I'll go in. Just try to keep quiet, okay? Because I think, you know, we're scaring her."

Jessie clamped her mouth shut and nodded her head yes. Evan stood for a minute outside the tepee, thinking. Then he undid the buckles on his snowshoes and stepped out of them, pulled back the tarp, and ducked inside.

Two summers ago, when they first built the tepee, Evan could stand inside at the tallest spot. But now his head butted up against the sloping branches that leaned against the center tree pole. He started to lean over, then realized it would be easier just to kneel on the ground. This brought him eye to eye with Grandma, and one look at her face told him she was very scared.

"Ma'am?" he said. "Are you waiting for the bus?"

"Yes!" she said. "I've been waiting for hours!" She looked so relieved then—almost happy—that Evan wished more than anything he could make a bus appear, right here in the middle of the woods.

"It isn't coming," he said. "There's been a problem. A flat tire. The bus can't make it here today."

"Well, send another!" said Grandma. "That's ridiculous. There's a bus every hour on this route. I've been taking this bus for years. I know the schedule."

"All the buses are broken," said Evan. "I'm sorry."

"That's inexcusable!" said Grandma. "I'm going to write a letter." The hand on her good arm started to pluck at her coat.

"Yes, you should," said Evan. "But right now, we have to get you home."

"Wait a minute. Who are you?" she asked suddenly.

"I work for the bus company. They told me to tell you that the bus isn't coming and that I should take you home."

"I've been waiting for hours!"

"I know," said Evan. "It's awful. You should write a letter."

"I'm going to!"

All the time they were talking, Evan slowly moved closer to Grandma. When he rested a hand on her arm, she didn't back away, and when he helped her to her feet, she leaned on his shoulder and went along.

"There's another passenger outside," said Evan. "She's been waiting for hours, too. Do you mind if she walks with us?"

"Inexcusable. You can't expect people to wait for hours. People depend on the bus. And what happened to the bench? Who took the bench?"

Evan ushered Grandma outside the tepee and nodded to Jessie, who had taken several steps back. "You know, kids probably," said Evan. "Kids do some really stupid things these days."

He put her arm over his shoulder and his hand on her back, then shone his flashlight on the snow ahead of them. Jessie walked right behind, but Grandma never once turned around to look at her.

Evan kept talking. Grandma seemed to think she was young again, in the days when she rode the bus three times a week to her classes at the community college. Every once in a while, she would stop walking and ask Evan, "Who are you again?" and Evan would remind her that he was with the bus company and it was his job to escort her home. Once she said, "I can't go home! I have to get to class!" But Evan told her that all the classes were canceled because of the snow. Grandma said she thought that was ridiculous, but she kept on walking.

When they reached the house, Evan could see his mother's car and Pete's truck parked out front. He suddenly felt so tired, he wanted to stop right where he was and lie down in the snow. Grandma, however, seemed to perk up when she saw the house in front of her.

"Thank you," she said, taking her arm off his shoulder and patting the front of his ski coat. "It was nice of you to walk me home. But you can go now." And she turned to go into the house.

Evan watched her walk up the stairs, knock the snow off her boots, and push open the front door. He could tell she knew exactly where she was. She was home.

"Evan?" said Jessie. "Is she okay?"

"Sure," said Evan. "Look at her. She's fine." He paused for a second. "She's just different than she was."

"Really different."

Evan shrugged. "Not all that different. Still Grandma." He took a few steps toward the house, then turned around. Jessie wasn't following. "C'mon. Let's go inside."

"No," said Jessie. "I need to go see Maxwell."

The picture came into Evan's mind of Maxwell

running like a wild animal, screaming as he went. It seemed to Evan as if there were an endless number of people to worry about. "You have to come inside first. Mom has to *see* you, to make sure you're okay."

Jessie nodded. Evan waved his arm toward the house. "C'mon. I'll walk you over to Maxwell's later."

Chapter 15
What's Wrong with Maxwell?

Evan kept his promise to her. But it took a while. First there was the commotion of Mrs. Treski hugging them both about a hundred times. Then Pete phoned the police to call off the search party. Then Evan told everyone how they'd found Grandma because *Jessie* had figured it out, because *Jessie* was so smart. She liked that part.

Then there was dinner, which was just canned soup and cold sandwiches because no one had the energy to cook a real meal but everyone was starving. And then Mrs. Treski said she wanted to get Grandma to bed early, never mind that it was New

Year's Eve. Which is when Jessie said she wanted to go see Maxwell, and Evan said he'd walk her over. The snow had stopped falling and a bright moon had broken through the clouds, so Mrs. Treski said yes. But be back soon.

When Maxwell's house came into view, Evan stopped on the path. "I'll wait back at the house, okay? Just call when you want to come home." Evan had never been inside Maxwell's house, so maybe he felt funny about going in.

Or maybe Evan just didn't want to talk to Maxwell's mom about what had happened that afternoon. Jessie could understand that.

She had hoped to avoid Mrs. Cooper altogether—somehow slip inside unnoticed. Maybe she wasn't even home? But instead, Maxwell's mom answered the door and asked Jessie to sit in the living room while she finished loading the dishwasher. Jessie sat down on the couch and looked at the photographs on top of the piano. There were dozens of them, and they were all of Maxwell.

Mrs. Cooper walked out of the kitchen, drying

her hands on a dishtowel. She sat on the couch next to Jessie. Usually, Jessie felt comfortable around grownups—sometimes more comfortable than with kids. But not this time.

Mrs. Cooper stared at her, with a look as hard as granite. "So. What happened this afternoon?"

Jessie took a minute to think. Should she tell the whole story? Or would Maxwell get in trouble? Had they broken any rules? What if she just left out the part about spying?

In the end, she figured the whole story was going to come out anyway. She might as well give it up now.

So she told Mrs. Cooper everything, from the very beginning. About the missing bell. And what Maxwell overheard on the bus. And the stakeout and how wrong it had gone. She described the frog and then the rock through the window and how Maxwell ran away screaming. Mrs. Cooper listened without saying a word.

When she was done talking, Jessie waited for Mrs. Cooper's response, but all she said was

"I wish those boys had never moved to the neighborhood."

"Me, too," said Jessie, thinking about the missing bell. She was sure the boys had it hidden somewhere. "But why is Maxwell afraid of them? He's bigger than they are."

"They tease him. Play mean jokes on him. About a month ago, they tricked Maxwell into climbing inside a cardboard moving box. They said it was a game. But instead of a game, they taped him up inside the box and left him like that—for hours. Maxwell doesn't like tight spaces."

"That's horrible," said Jessie. She couldn't imagine being trapped like that. It made her legs and arms feel twitchy just to think about it.

Mrs. Cooper looked across the room, then shook her head slowly. "They're just *mean* boys."

They sure were. But why? Were they born that way? Were some people born one way and some people another?

"You can go see Maxwell now, if you want," said Mrs. Cooper, standing up and snapping the dishtowel over her shoulder. "He's in his room playing a video game."

Jessie jumped off the couch and headed for the stairs that led down to the basement, which was where Maxwell's bedroom was. She was on the third step when she stopped and turned around. "Mrs. Cooper?" said Jessie. "What's wrong with Maxwell?"

Mrs. Cooper paused in the doorway to the kitchen and looked at her. "He's just different, that's all. He sees things differently than we do. He feels the world in a different way, too. Things bother him that wouldn't you or me, like loud noises or changes in his routine or new people. To us, they're no big deal, but to Maxwell, they're a very big deal. And even though Maxwell's incredibly smart, there are some things he has trouble understanding. Like feelings. He has a really tough time understanding feelings."

"Oh," said Jessie.

Like me, she thought.

She found Maxwell leaning against the giant gorilla pillow that sat at the head of his bed. The arms of the gorilla wrapped around Maxwell, as if the big furry ape were trying to reach the game controller Maxwell held in his hands.

Maxwell didn't even look up when Jessie walked in.

"Hey," she said.

Maxwell nodded his head, his eyes never leaving the screen.

Jessie stared at the TV. The game was one of those questing games, where dwarves and dragons and giants and other magical characters fight each other and collect treasure. Pretty soon she was sitting on the edge of the bed, as caught up in the game as Maxwell was.

"Can I try?" asked Jessie.

"No, I'm right in the middle of a quest. Later."

"When, later?"

"When I die."

"When are you going to die?"

Maxwell shrugged. "Probably not for a while. I'm really good at this game."

Jessie watched the treasure points pile up on the

counter in the upper-right corner of the screen. Maxwell's character, a twinkly-eyed dwarf with a mohawk, seemed invincible. He killed a dragon, two evil elf twins, and a giant with a weapon that could shoot lightning bolts.

"I wish we'd had one of those when Jeff and Mike tried to hurt that frog," said Jessie.

Maxwell nodded his head. "I would have killed them both."

"You're not supposed to want to kill people in real life," she said, but she knew what he meant. She really didn't like those boys. And even though Evan and Jessie and Maxwell had managed to save the frog, she knew that the Sinclair boys would do something just as awful again someday. Who would be around then to stand up to them?

Besides that, Jessie was sure they had the bell—hidden in the barn or stashed under the porch or maybe buried out in the woods. "Do you think they've got it?" she asked Maxwell. "The bell, I mean?"

"Nope," said Maxwell, punching furiously on

the controller buttons. It was amazing how fast he was. Jessie watched as his dwarf decapitated a black-robed warlock.

"Why not?"

"Because I know where it is."

Jessie continued looking at the screen, not understanding what Maxwell had just said. Was he talking about something in the game? Maybe he didn't get what she was talking about.

"You know where *what* is?"

"The bell," said Maxwell. "Dang!" He pointed at the screen. "I lost a life, but I can buy it back." Ten thousand points fell off the counter, and Maxwell's dead dwarf jumped to his feet and started fighting again.

"You know where the bell is?" Jessie's voice was weirdly quiet. She felt like she'd walked into a mental hospital, and you were not supposed to yell in hospitals.

"Yep."

"Where is it?" Her voice grew a little louder.

"In my closet."

"In your *closet?"* Jessie jumped off the bed and pushed open the sliding door to the closet. On the floor was a laundry basket, an old box filled with LEGO pieces, and Grandma's bell.

"Why did you steal Grandma's bell?" Now Jessie was yelling.

"I didn't steal it. I protected it. Mrs. Joyce was in the hospital for a whole week. I didn't want Jeff and Mike to take it like they said they would. So I took it down and hid it in my closet."

"But . . . but . . . why didn't you tell me that?"

"Because you didn't ask."

"But . . . you knew I was looking for it! When someone's looking for something and you know where it is, you tell them!"

Maxwell kept playing his game. "You said it was a puzzle. You said you like to solve puzzles by yourself. I thought you wanted to figure it out on your own."

"But you can't just take something from someone without telling them. That's *stealing."*

"Is not. I told Mrs. Joyce. I told her when I visited

her in the hospital. I guess she forgot."

Well, duh! thought Jessie.

She stared at the bell. It looked just like it always had. Except it was sitting on the floor of Maxwell's closet! She really did feel like the whole world had gone crazy and left her behind—the only sane person on the planet. She couldn't think of what to say. "You're really . . . you're . . ."

"Smart," said Maxwell. "I'm Maxwell, and I'm smart."

Jessie looked at Maxwell, who was still furiously playing the video game, killing gnomes and druids left and right. It was just like his mother had said: Maxwell was different.

She grabbed hold of the top of the bell and tried to pull on it, to see how heavy it really was. The bell tilted, but there was no way she could lift it.

"Well, if you're so smart," said Jessie, "then tell me how we're going to get this bell out of your basement and hanging up on the hill by tonight."

Chapter 16
Ring Out, Wild Bells

Pete would have been proud. That's what Evan thought as he neared the top of Lovell's Hill. There was the bell, hanging on the crossbeam, the way it had for as long as Evan could remember. Something about seeing it there gave him such a sense of gratitude and happiness that he reached out his arm and put it around Jessie's shoulder, giving her a quick squeeze as they climbed the last few steps to the top.

"It's still here," said Jessie. As if anyone could have gotten it down again! Evan, Maxwell, and Jessie had spent two hours hauling the bell back up the hill on a toboggan with only the moon lighting their way. Then they'd hoisted it onto the hooks and lashed it to the crossbeam with a rope that Jessie tied in a million knots. When they were done hanging the bell, Evan had noticed a few spots on the post that were splintered. Tomorrow, he would come up here with a sanding block and work on the wood until it was smooth, just the way Pete had taught him.

Evan nodded. "Still here." It was good to know that the bell would remain, right where it belonged.

The snow that had fallen earlier carpeted the hillside, and the moon shone brightly in the clear, cold air. The effect was like a stadium lit up for a night game. Evan could see all kinds of details: the letters inscribed on the bell, the grain in the wood of the crossbeam, and the faces of the people gathered. Some of them he recognized, like Mrs. Upton and the Bradleys, who had been friends of Grandma's for years. But lots of the people were new to Evan.

Grandma would have known them all, but Grandma was home resting with Mom. Evan was sorry about that. It didn't feel like New Year's Eve without Grandma.

Of course, Maxwell was there with his mom and dad, all three on cross-country skis. When he spotted Evan and Jessie, Maxwell *whooshed* over to them. He held up his wrist with its digital watch.

"Twelve minutes and thirty-eight seconds. Exactly," he said. "I set my watch to the official NIST clock. It's accurate to within six-tenths of a second." Then he *whooshed* back over to his parents, who were talking to a young couple Evan didn't recognize. The man was holding a small child in his arms and had his back to Evan. The woman was someone Evan had never seen before.

"I guess we know who the youngest is this year," said Evan to Jessie, pointing at the couple.

Jessie looked over at them and said, "I didn't know Pete had a kid!"

"That's not—" but then Evan looked closer and

saw that it *was* Pete. "I didn't know, either!" Evan walked over, feeling a little shy. "Hey," he said to Pete. "Man of the family, huh?"

Pete broke into a smile and put out his fist for Evan to bump. "You know it. This is my posse. Kayley, say hi to Big Man Evan." But the little girl in Pete's arms just buried her face against her dad's shoulder, too shy and sleepy to greet a stranger. "And this is my wife, Melissa."

Evan said hello and shook hands politely, the way he'd been taught. Melissa told him how relieved she was to hear that Grandma was okay. "You and your sister are heroes," she said.

Evan looked at Pete, and Pete raised his eyebrows in response. He'd already given Evan a talking-to in private about not sticking to the plan they'd agreed on. *Traipsing off in the woods and dragging your little sister with you!* But Evan could tell by the way Pete smiled now that he was just as glad as Melissa that Grandma had been found, safe and sound.

"All's well that ends well," said Melissa, tucking the leg of Kayley's snow pants into her boot. "Too bad she couldn't be here, though. It won't be the same without her."

They stood in the moonlight, talking about the events of the day and the trip home planned for tomorrow. Evan and Jessie and Mrs. Treski were driving back in the morning, and Grandma would be coming with them. Maybe for good. Pete would keep working on the house. He thought he'd have it all wrapped up by the end of January.

There was a pause in the conversation, and then Melissa asked, "So who's the oldest?" They all looked around, and a murmur began to sweep through the crowd. *Who's the oldest this year?* One man said, "I'm fifty-three," and a woman called out, "Fifty-eight, here." "Where's Mrs. Lewis?" asked someone, and a voice in the crowd said, "She's staying home. Said to say hello to everyone."

"Not so many of the older folks this year," said Pete. "On account of the snow, I guess."

Evan shook his head. If Grandma were here, she'd have them all beat by a couple of decades.

"Four minutes!" yelled Maxwell. "Precisely!"

Everyone on the hill began to crowd in closer, forming a warm circle around the New Year's Eve bell. "Another year!" shouted someone, and Mrs. Cooper said, "And not a day wiser!" which made people laugh. Evan watched as Pete moved into the very center of the circle, holding Kayley close to him and whispering in her ear. The woman who had announced her age as fifty-eight also moved into the center of the circle and said something to Pete that made him throw back his head and laugh.

"C'mon, Jess," said Evan. His sister was hanging on the outside of the circle, staring at the path that led back to the house. "What are you waiting for?"

"Three minutes!" shouted Maxwell.

Suddenly Jessie broke away from the circle and started running toward the woods. "It's Grandma. She's here. She made it!"

Everyone in the circle turned to look. It really was Grandma! Evan couldn't believe it. And his mother was right behind her.

Jessie had already grabbed hold of Grandma's good arm and was pulling her toward the circle.

A cheer rose up from the crowd as everyone on the hill burst into muffled mittened applause. The sound bounced off Black Bear Mountain and ricocheted back to the top of Lovell's Hill.

"Two minutes, thirty seconds!" shouted Maxwell.

"I'm guessing I'm the oldest?" said Grandma, breathing hard as she broke through the circle.

"Yes, ma'am," said Pete. "And Kayley here's the youngest."

"Well, then we're good to go!" said Grandma. "Except—" She looked around her, searching the crowd. "Except this year, I want—" She spotted Maxwell and waved him over. "Maxwell. And Jessie, you, too. And . . . and . . ."

"Grandma, we can't all ring the bell," said Jessie. "It's not the tradition!"

"I don't care!" said Grandma. "This year I want something different. I want . . ." She continued to look at each face in the crowd. Evan shuffled his feet uncomfortably. Grandma's eyes finally came to rest on his face. "You!" she said. "Come here. I want you here, too."

Evan walked forward, miserably. It was awful to be forgotten by Grandma at all, but even worse to have it happen in front of so many people. It made him feel like he had done something bad, something he was being punished for.

Grandma grabbed his shoulder with her good hand and pulled him in close to her. She bent her face down so that her forehead touched his. In the bright moonlight, he could see the spidery wrinkles around her mouth, the fine lines that trickled from her eyes. Her face looked frightened. He was frightened, too. What would she do? What would she say?

"I do know you," she whispered. "I do. I just can't . . . I can't quite put it all together. But I *know* you."

Evan nodded his head. "It's okay, Grandma. It's okay."

"Ten, nine, eight . . ." shouted Maxwell, his face lit up green by the glow of his digital watch.

They had to crowd together: Pete, holding Kayley, Evan, Jessie, Maxwell, and Grandma, each one grabbing a few inches of the rope that hung from the bell's heavy clapper.

Everyone on the hill joined in the countdown. ". . . five, four, three, two, one!"

Evan swung his hand back and forth wildly. The five of them pulled in different directions, and the first few peals of the bell were weak and halting. But then they found a rhythm, and they swung the rope back and forth in perfect unison, until the noise of the bell filled the snow-covered valley below and the echoes of each peal bounced off of Black Bear Mountain and came racing back to them.

Evan listened to the bell and thought that it sounded different this year. Maybe because he was ringing it? Maybe because it had been taken down and then hung again? It sounded lower, a little bit sadder. Then he listened again and thought, no, it sounded the same as always.

Different and the same.

In Pete's arms, Kayley pumped her legs wildly

and then threw her head back and crowed at the night sky.

"You don't see that every day!" shouted Maxwell, and Grandma laughed just like she used to, loud and rumbly.

Evan smiled at Jessie, and she smiled back at him. "Happy New Year, Jess!" he shouted, above the wild clamor of the bell.

"I SOUND THE ALARM
TO KEEP THE PEACE."
New Year's
Jessie Treski